Intriguing  interspersed ... Frank King's *Travels with Doris* a rich read. Whether unveiling the mysteries of ankle bracelets in India or reveling in an unexpected paradise in the jungles of Guatemala, this is travel adventure with a heart. Hop on board with this seventy-something couple; you'll cheer their sweet romance and admire the indomitable spirit of Doris as she captures hearts across the world. Travels with Doris is a delight.

Michelle Roedell, editor, Northwest Prime Time

A wry account of travels off the beaten track—far off, of an ever loving, ever sparing couple as described from the bemused, often perplexed and humbled, occasionally irreverent viewpoint of one, Mr. Frank King. It's a joy to read about Frank and Doris, albeit later in life, but none the less full of romance as it blossoms through the rigors and serendipitous discoveries of travel on the wild side. The stories of this globetrotting couple make for a good read anywhere you may be perched; hammock, train seat, armchair, dentist office.

Debbie Anderson, Mountaineer, traveler

Frank King and his wife, Doris, travel in a way most of us wish we could; no reservations, without tours or guides, and only a small backpack. You might imagine them as well under forty, but add about thirty years to these carefree spirits. They go to meet and mingle with the ordinary people wherever they find themselves. These vividly told stories reflect the author's love of humanity, Doris' gutsy attitude, and a wonderful sense of humor.

Lenore Ziontz, author of: The Hour of Lead

Part travelogue, all love stories, *Travels with Doris* traces Frank King and his partner, Doris, as they journey to different parts of the world. Carrying small backpacks and completely on their own, their love of travel and the enjoyment of people and places they encounter come alive. They are the sort of traveling couple we all hope to meet.

Matt Huston, educator and vicarious adventurer

Here's an intriguing love story based on carefree world-wide travels.

*Peter Tower, former owner and CEO,
C J Tower and Son, customhouse broker*

Frank King has laid down a very well written, thus easy to read, post-retirement memoir of travel and adventure from our own Cascades to the wilds of South America and Africa, the cultural shock of India, and the civility of Europe. Might make the reader want to pack up and head out.

*Shelby Scates,
author of: War and Politics by Other Means*

Travels with Doris

To those who read this book ~
Have fun & adventures traveling with us through the pages of this book.

Frank

Have fun following your dreams, I did.
Doris

Travels with Doris

Without Reservations

FRANK KING

Tate Publishing & *Enterprises*

Travels with Doris
Copyright © 2009 by Frank King. All rights reserved.

No part of this publication may be reproduced, stored in a retrieval system or transmitted in any way by any means, electronic, mechanical, photocopy, recording or otherwise without the prior permission of the author except as provided by USA copyright law.

Names, descriptions, entities, and incidents included in the story are based on the lives of real people.

The opinions expressed by the author are not necessarily those of Tate Publishing, LLC.

Published by Tate Publishing & Enterprises, LLC
127 E. Trade Center Terrace | Mustang, Oklahoma 73064 USA
1.888.361.9473 | www.tatepublishing.com

Tate Publishing is committed to excellence in the publishing industry. The company reflects the philosophy established by the founders, based on Psalm 68:11,
"The Lord gave the word and great was the company of those who published it."

Book design copyright © 2009 by Tate Publishing, LLC. All rights reserved.
Cover design by Amber Lee
Interior design by Stephanie Woloszyn

Published in the United States of America

ISBN: 978-1-60696-138-4
1. Travel / Special Interest / Senior
2. Biography & Autobiography / Personal Memoirs
09.03.03

Table of Contents

Introduction	9
The First Journey: Italy	13
Bangles and Bracelets: India	29
At Play Among Scary Animals: Botswana	39
A Road Trip without Roads: Paraguay & Bolivia	53
Bringing in the Hay: Switzerland	71
Guatemala through a Side Door	79
A Zipper among the Roses: Czech Republic	95
Riding the Rails in India	101
The Fiesta at Coixtlahuaca, Mexico	115
Sleeping Well in Dracula's Town, Romania	127
Sleeping Better in Dracula's Town: Romania	139
Jeep across the Andes: Bolivia to Chile	153
Bloody Hell, Americans: South Africa	173
Biking Through History: Ireland	179
Trekking the Tatras: Slovakia	195
A Party for Shiva: India	213
Travel Angels: Czech Republic	223

Doris Gets Deported—Almost: Paraguay	229
Holy Wells of Ireland	247
Romanian Hospitality	251
More Romanian Hospitality	263
A Romanian Excursion	277
Epilogue	289

Introduction

I was damaged goods in my mid-sixties when, for fun, I began flirting with Doris on a trip to Italy. She was an older woman by one year. But I had fun anyway despite our great age difference; hiking, climbing, and talking–lots of talking. In the process, I told her about my defects; warts and all. Yet, she accepted me as is, the whole packaged deal, and took me home with her anyway. That was the start of my travels with Doris.

Long before Doris, I received the first warning of my mortality at the age of fifty seven. I went in for an angioplasty, a method of opening clogged arteries feeding the heart. I didn't realize it, and my doctor didn't say, but I had started on a long slide downhill that included four angioplasties plus a heart attack. Then came open-heart surgery, and a little later, the final insult–the implanting of a defibrillator/pacemaker in my chest. I was also an insulin junkie combating diabetes. So, when I started my travels with Doris, I was definitely damaged goods.

Doris had a major defect too, which remained hidden until the day she tried to step across a big log and got stuck halfway across. Not able to move forward or back because of the pain, she laughed like crazy at her predicament.

"What's the matter?" I asked.

"It's my hip," she said grimacing from either pain or humor, I couldn't tell which. "It's all worn out and sometimes it locks up. My doctor says I'll need a hip replacement someday."

"It looks like you need it now," I said, watching her maneuver to a sitting position and, with the help of her hands, swing her other leg over the log.

"Oh no. It only hurts sometimes going over a big log like this one, or at the end of a long hike."

She finally did get a hip replacement, at seventy four; and to my disgust, I could no longer keep up with her. Despite our frailties, we backpacked in the Grand Canyon, biked in Ireland, and paddled our kayak in Puget Sound. But best of all, we traveled to many foreign countries. I've always planned the itineraries for those trips very carefully, knowing full well my limitations and the risks I took in traveling with only two-thirds of my heart working properly. By my mid-seventies, I had to give up on the strenuous activities, but traveling was still something I could do well.

Doris was the perfect traveling companion. She had a sunny disposition, loved to talk, and took a genuine interest in the people she met. I planned the trips, and she cheerfully followed. Yet, she was the one who found the friends, took all the pictures, and wrote copious notes. She remembered people and places better than I, but still had to ask me where in the world they were.

We traveled everywhere with a light backpack, hopefully keeping the weight under twenty-five pounds.

To maintain spontaneity, we seldom made reservations for a place to stay at night.

I kept warning Doris, saying, "Some night we might end up on a park bench."

"Don't worry," she replied, "there'll always be a place for us to stay."

She was right, but we've had some close calls.

Our trips normally start and end with an international flight, in and out of the same city. The land part of the itinerary follows a big loop, with stops along the way, using as many daylong and overnight bus or train rides as it takes to complete the loop.

The stories that follow are unrelated and in no special order. The only continuity among them is Doris, myself, and the universal kindness of people we've met the world over.

Doris finds me on a mountain in Italy.

The First Journey: Italy

Doris likes to tell friends and strangers that she found me on a mountaintop in Italy and brought me home with her. That might bring to mind an unlikely scene of Doris, at age sixty seven, stumbling over my body on top of a mountain and stuffing me in her big, pink duffel bag to take home as a souvenir of her Italian trip. Normally, I don't say anything, because it's her fun. But sometimes I set the record straight and tell people exactly what happened that fall in 1995.

Actually, I met Doris two weeks before the Italy trip. I went on a climb of Silver Peak in the Cascade Mountains with thirteen other Seattle Mountaineers, a group of hikers and climbers going overseas for two weeks as guests of the Italian Alpine Club, known as CAI. Diane, our leader, organized the climb as a way for everyone to get acquainted. Doris was one of the few people I didn't know, so I made it a point to get acquainted with her.

She was nice, and fun to be with. She had a laugh you could hear a mile away, a sunny disposition, and loved to talk. But her legs attracted me more than anything else. I barely glanced at her above the waist. Those beautiful, hard brown legs were wonderful to watch, and I exerted myself to keep up with them. As a result, I strode down that mountain going like the blazes, passing everyone in sight.

That evening, Eddie, my good climbing friend, held a potluck at his house where our group could discuss the trip and learn more details. I think we did talk about the trip, a little, but between the glasses of wine and watching Doris in shorts, I don't remember. I still had a terrible time making eye contact with her, because of those darn pretty legs. That evening, we all parted ways, and because my departure was delayed by my work schedule, I didn't see any of them again until I arrived in the village of Liviglioni, Italy where they had arrived three days earlier.

Liviglioni is a small village perched part way up one of the peaks that make up the Apennine Alps lying between Pisa and Milano. To get there, I changed trains twice from Rome. Then I rode a bus that wheezed its way up steep slopes to where it finally gave-up and dropped me off a mile below the village. From there, I hiked the road uphill to the hotel. The gang of Seattle Mountaineers had just returned from a daylong hike, and gave me passing greetings as they disappeared to get cleaned-up for supper.

I shared a room with Mark, the youngest person on the trip. He was a big muscular-looking kid in his mid-thirties, the youngest of the group, who turned out to be a total cream puff. Neither of us wanted to share the large comfortable bed in the room. My skin crawled when I thought about it. Fortunately, the room had a small daybed in one corner, and we reached an agreement to trade beds each night. His most annoying habit was loud snoring all night. Worse, he periodically stopped breathing. Wide-eyed, I'd lay there awake waiting for him to start breathing and snoring again. He always did, but I wondered what I would do if he didn't.

That night at supper, I sat with the others at one long table strewn with red and white wine in bottles that never ran dry. Luckily, I got a seat across from Doris, and that's how I found out she looked pretty good from the waist up, too. Wonderful smells of cooking meat came from the kitchen, and soon dinner came out in great bowls of spaghetti and meatballs. It was so good I had seconds and was disappointed when the bowls disappeared before I could get thirds. *The Italian's must eat light meals*, I thought. Then came the real dinner, three kinds of meat and roasted veggies served family style–all you could eat. And then salad followed by desert. Stuffed from eating too much, I could hardly waddle out of the dining room.

I met Doris at the entry of the hotel where we had agreed during dinner to meet for a walk around the village, alone. I wanted to pursue my interest in her sparked by our first meeting when we climbed Silver Peak back home. But how can you sneak out when a dozen eyes follow your every move? As we walked, we made an easy adjustment to hold hands, and then graduated to arms around each other. But as I was about to make the grand move aiming for a spontaneous kiss, the whole gang from dinner came charging along, greeting us like long lost friends. They gaily walked us back to the hotel, and we downgraded to just holding hands again.

The next day, I hiked and climbed with the others, but ended up spending a lot of time near Doris with both of us pretending our involvement was just coincidental. We talked about anything and everything. I learned about her husband dying ten years before, and her twenty-nine-year-old son dying of a brain tumor eight months before that. She told me about her move to Seattle to be close to her daughter and the grandchildren. Then, I told Doris about Susan and our divorce. And how, after that, Susan and I lived together for the next nineteen years, slowly growing further apart to the point we now slept in separate rooms, living together out of habit and too lazy to make a change. Susan was gone a lot, visiting her daughter and grandson in Montana, and I spent a lot of time alone in a dusty, empty house. I told Doris that last part to gain a little sympathy and maybe get her to overlook that I was still living with Susan.

That evening I got to the dining room early and picked out a seat hoping Doris would sit across from me again. She did. This time I was smarter, and didn't load-up on the starter course; I waited for the real meal to come.

After supper, Eddie, with Diane's urging, started a sing-a-long. They both liked to sing, and I did too. We were just getting warmed-up when several Italian men in the next room suddenly adjourned their meeting and joined us to sing along. Magically, two guitars appeared to accompany the singing. Soon we were trading American songs and Italian songs and having a great time. The

Italian songs were familiar tunes, but I didn't know the words. A few of our songs, like "Oh Susanna," "You Are My Sunshine," and "Clementine" were well known by the Italians and we all gave lusty renditions of those.

A few of our Italian hosts, members of the Italian Alpine Club, CAI, started dancing. Some of the other Italian men moved all the tables, except the ones where we sat, to one side of the room and piled the chairs on top. Pretty soon, everyone, including Doris and I, were dancing while a few hard-core singers and the guitarists continued the music-making process. It didn't matter if you had a partner or not, everyone danced anyway. Even the kitchen help and the cooks joined in, as well as some of the hotel staff and other guests. With no lack of wine, the impromptu party lasted for hours. Those Italians were tireless, but we weren't. They danced wildly about the dining room with or without partners, clapped hands, and sang, all the while drinking endless bottles of wine.

Doris and I finally sneaked off to the second floor hallway where we attempted to exchange some kisses in the dark. To my disgust, the entire Seattle contingent decided to go to bed, too. Every time we got a good start, someone would turn on the lights, climb the stairs, and bid us a cheery good night on the way to their room. Finally, we gave up and went to bed where I had to endure Mark's snoring interspersed with his silent periods. It was my turn on the little daybed, and I tossed and turned for hours before falling asleep with the sounds of merrymaking still coming from the dining room. *Boy, those Italians liked to party.*

The next day was an easy hiking day. Doris and I tried to maintain the appearance of just normal friends who happened to sit together a lot and talk together a lot. I don't think we fooled anyone. That afternoon we went to a chestnut roasting party. Underneath the canopy of big chestnut trees several tables were laid with snacks and finger food but mostly wine bottles covered the tables as our Italian hosts brought their family labels for us to try. They were proud of their homemade wine and urged us to try different ones, sort of like a wine tasting party, but using full glasses of wine.

Smoke from an open fire drifted about leaving its scent behind. Under our feet dry leaves crackled and swished bringing out the bittersweet scent of fall. Chestnuts littered the ground, and many of them were roasting on the fire in oversized frying pans with handles a yard long. We gorged on chestnuts, which I had never eaten before, and drank the wine. Almost all of it was red and I saw no difference in the taste of their homemade wine than that of the any of the wines I'd bought at home. At some point the singing burst out, and I think maybe we were all a little tipsy. Diane ended the party abruptly, because, as she announced to us, our hotel staff was expecting us back for dinner. I groaned at the thought of eating another one of their gargantuan meals.

When Doris and I got back to the hotel, Diane and her permanent partner, Jim, invited us to sit with them and ordered us a drink. The last thing I wanted was another drink, but what the heck; she was the leader.

Without any preamble, she said to me, "I'm making

some room changes. I'm moving Mark out of your room, and I would like Doris to move in with you. Doris needs a bigger room and you can do without Mark's snoring. I've already told Mark to move."

How did she know Mark snored?

Doris said, "Okay," and she left to pack-up.

I sat silently a few seconds, with a foolish grin on my face, wondering how this good fortune had come about. Finally, I said, "Diane, you know I'm a team player when it comes to outings like this. If you feel the group would be better off with Doris in my room, I certainly will agree to the change."

"I know, it's a terrible sacrifice," she said laughing. "But quit messing with us and get going before I change my mind."

When I got to my room, I had to step around a strange suitcase parked in front of the door. That's when I knew Doris was a fast woman. *Kind of neat,* I thought.

For Doris and me the meal that evening was an unending process, each of us looking forward to being together alone. At last it was over, and we could leave our group without appearing too hasty. Inside our room, we could hardly contain our excitement, finally free from chaperones and all alone.

But what now? We started with hugs and kisses, and that was fun. Then came a delicate discussion of sleeping arrangements. After all, two beds were in the room. We quickly decided to use the bigger more comfortable bed even though that meant sleeping together with all its ramifications.

But now what? Suddenly I was aware of the big elephant in the room—SEX. Strangely I hadn't yet thought of that aspect of being with Doris and was unsure of what to do next. As if reading my mind, Doris explained that she hadn't slept with a man in more then ten years, since her husband died.

Twisting her hands tightly in her lap and staring intently at her feet, she said in a low voice, " I'm not sure I want to try, at least not yet."

"Well, that's a relief," I replied, "since my heart attack six years ago and because of all the drugs I take, I haven't been able to have sex either."

With these disclosures we found it easier to get undressed and ready for bed, since neither of us had to perform, sexually. To save ourselves any potential embarrassment we slipped into bed still partly clothed, me in underwear, and Doris in an oversized T-shirt which I found very intriguing. We spent the whole night slowly learning how to please each other in spite of my disability and her fears. It was easier than I thought it would be, but then, I figured most sex was in the mind anyway. We messed around, had a lot of fun, and learned a lot about each other in a very short time. And we were awake to hear that noisy bell from the town clock strike every hour and half-hour throughout the night.

In the morning, I left the room before Doris in the hope of preserving a little propriety. But most of the group wasn't fooled; I noticed their knowing looks and half-smiles. Then, Diane came in with a big grin and asked in voice loud enough for the whole world to hear,

"Well, did you sleep good last night? It must have been quiet without Mark's snoring."

"Sure I did," I mumbled.

"That's good, because we have a big strenuous climb ahead of us today."

I groaned to myself. Actually, I was exhausted from being up all night. Somehow, I had to get through the day's activities, no matter how hard that might be. A just atonement for sins came to mind, but only briefly, as Doris came in to stand by me.

We left Liviglioni the next day to proceed on with the scheduled itinerary. Our CAI hosts had arranged places for us to stay based on the information given to them weeks before we left Seattle. Each night, Doris and I stayed with a different Italian host until the last day of the outing, where we got to share a home-stay in Milano. In the meantime, I had this wonderful idea of how to get Doris and I to know one another better.

"Would you like to go to Sicily after this outing is over?" I asked. "It'll be warm and sunny, and there are lots of things to see and do, like forts and palaces, and poking about ruins. There are also great shops." I threw that last in, attempting to be more persuasive.

I expected the usual womanly reply of: "I don't think so," "Well, maybe," "Let me think about it," "I'll let you know in the morning," or, just a plain, "No."

Instead, she said, "I'll have to change my plane ticket to go home at a later date. How long do you think we'll need?"

Stunned by my good fortune, I muttered something

about needing two or three weeks, but I don't remember. I figured we each could spare the extra time. After all, we were supposed to be retired. Adding up our money we had enough for the trip to Sicily if we traveled frugally, and I was very good at doing that.

That last night in Milano was a feverish time of activity for Doris. I took one look at the huge pink duffel bag, suitcase, and backpack she carried around and laid down an ultimatum.

"If you're going to travel with me, you must get all the stuff you need in your backpack, and ship everything else home. Don't worry; I'm good at this, so I can help you."

I always had an easier time eliminating other peoples stuff than my own, but I didn't tell Doris that.

She agonized over the things to take and pleaded for mercy, but I was strong for once, and insisted she take only her backpack and whatever she could cram into it. At some point during the evening when she wasn't looking, I cinched her pack to a smaller size. I was hoping her pack would weigh in at about twenty-five pounds when completely stuffed. At that weight, I knew she would have an easier time carrying her pack around and hoisting it up into the luggage racks on trains and busses.

In the morning we went to the train station, each of us carrying one pack on our backs. I noticed she had cheated a little and carried a small daypack in her hands. When I asked about it, she replied, "It's things I need during the day, and I'll never ask you to carry it for me."

Defiance? This was close to mutiny, I thought.

I quickly backed off. From then on, in all our travels

together throughout the world, she always carried a small second bag. Out of that second bag came food, water, books, toilet paper, and other neat things, all of which benefited me too.

Doris kicks up her heels on a mountain climb.

On our own at last, I found that traveling alone with Doris was exhilarating and fun. We both liked the trains, and the spontaneity of traveling without reservations. She never worried about where we were going or where we would sleep. I was left to worry about those things, and we both shared the same philosophy of sleeping cheap, not wanting to pay extravagant prices for a room, just to sleep.

In Sienna, she and I picnicked on roast chicken and a bottle of wine in its famous plaza. We sat on the cobblestones where sunlight and shadow met in a straight line across the center of the plaza. Doris liked sunshine; I preferred shade, and we solved our first incompatibility by

FRANK KING

Diane looks on while I open another bottle of wine at the chestnut roasting party.

sitting where sunshine and shadow met. We kept shifting position as the sun moved, since each of us wanted to stay in our comfort zone, but not sit too far from each other. That night we bought food from a Deli and ate in our hotel room, discovering we both liked Brussels sprouts. I divided them evenly between us, and then to maintain tranquility, cut the odd one in half. By traveling together we quickly learned each others' likes and dislikes, what made us feel good or bad, and how to please one another.

Sicily was sunny most of the time, but downright cold. At Enna, heavy snow fell as we tried to visit an old hilltop fortress. We couldn't see much in the blizzard and returned to our hotel early. Too early. The staff didn't offer much sympathy, but told us the heat came on later, maybe early in the evening. We took a hot shower and jumped in bed with all the blankets we could find in order to stay warm until dinnertime. We did that many times during our stay in Sicily. That's where I lost all my credibility with Doris concerning whether a place would be hot or cold. Fortunately, one of the items she had with her was a silk underwear top that she wore everyday while in Sicily. From then on, wherever we traveled, even in the tropics, Doris carried that darn silk underwear with her. She claimed it kept her warmer than me, but I never believed that.

Wanting to stay in Piazza Armerina to visit the ruins of a third century Roman villa located nearby, we looked at the last room available in the only hotel in town. The room had eight tiny beds lined up on one wall, kind of like where Snow White's seven dwarfs might stay.

"No way you silly man," Doris muttered to herself, referring to the manager who showed us the room.

"But Doris, there's no other rooms here," I said.

"How about out near the ruins?"

Checking the guidebook, I found a small hotel about three miles out of town on the way to the ruins.

"Let's go there," she said. "But no taxi. They're always way too expensive."

We tried hitchhiking, but ended up walking the entire distance, carrying our packs. Eventually, we arrived at a family-run inn that was more a home than inn. With no heat on in the house, Granddad sat in a big overstuffed chair wrapped to the chin in a blanket watching TV. Children chased merrily about in the cold dining room, and the harassed mom took us upstairs to show us a room with a cold radiator that she had available. Apparently the only warm place in the inn was the kitchen.

We got the room easily since we were the only guests. I laughed out loud when I saw the two single beds decorously separated by a nightstand. Doris muttered something about Italian morals and promptly pushed the two beds together. Later, she complained that she spent most of the night caught in the crack between the two beds. I discounted her complaint, because by now I had learned that Doris sometimes exaggerated.

That afternoon, we walked another one and one-half mile to the well-preserved ruins of a villa where Marcus Aurelius may have lived. The villa's real claim to fame were the mosaics, three thousand square feet of them, discovered in 1950 after being buried in mud for seven hundred years.

Eventually, our travels together had to end, and Doris cried a little on the train back to Milano to catch her plane. I still had over a week to go.

"Don't cry," I said, "we'll travel together again."

When she was gone, I missed her laughter and endless chatter, her hugs and kisses, and her feisty independence. I missed her company and called her every night wishing she was with me. Somehow, traveling alone wasn't as much fun, like it used to be.

She insisted on meeting me at the Vancouver Airport when I got back. At first, I didn't recognize her in that bright red plaid miniskirt, but then, I saw those beautiful brown legs.

She gave me a present in a little flat box wrapped in a bright red ribbon, and insisted I open it right there. When I did, I found a key, the key to her house.

Without words and at great risk, she offered me a change in my life. Silently I accepted, and we held each other tight a few seconds while my eyes blurred with a few pesky tears. Then, arm in arm, we walked out of that place to her car, and she drove all the way home. To our home.

Bangles and Bracelets: India

Something woke me from a sound sleep. I listened for a few seconds, not fully awake; all I heard was the rhythmic clicking of the coach wheels on the rails beneath the floor. The coach was stuffy, but by now the heat of the day before had dissipated and the temperature was at least bearable. There it was again, the noise I heard in my dream. Then, I realized Doris was having some kind of trouble. What I was hearing was her muttering and thrashing about, almost inaudible above the rumbling of wheels on the rails and the rattling of the ceiling fan in its wire cage.

She was on the top berth across the aisle and out of my sight from where I lay in the lower berth. Our beds, without bedding, were simply padded sleeping platforms that converted into seats during the day. I saw the Indian ladies across from me in the lower and middle berths. They were sleeping on their sides wrapped in their shawls, each with her head pillowed on one arm. I had lost the battle of an open window to them earlier and had to endure the hot sticky confines of my lower berth throughout the night.

I swung my feet into the aisle and quickly got up, cracking my head on the middle berth. Rats, I always forgot that the distance between the sleeping platforms was too small for a person to sit up straight unless they were children. I saw my reflection in the window still black with night, but the eternal light from the single bulb in the ceiling provided enough dim lighting to see around the compartment. Doris lay on the berth, knees bent, trying to reach her feet with her hands. The headroom on the top berth didn't allow her to sit up, so she twisted and turned on her side contorting her body in a desperate effort to reach that far.

I braced myself in the swaying coach with my head close to her face, and whispered, "What's the matter? Are you okay?"

"No, I'm not okay," she whispered back, loud enough to be heard in the next compartment. She continued twisting and turning, awkwardly trying to fumble with the bracelet she wore around each ankle.

"They're stuck together, and I can't get the darn things loose. And I can't move my legs. And I need to go to the bathroom, damn it."

She said this a little louder than a whisper, and I figured everyone else in the compartment was awake by now. But no one stirred. The Indian people were a polite bunch, figuring we would eventually solve our problem, whatever it was, and go back to sleep.

"What do you mean stuck?" I asked, stifling a desire to laugh. "Here I'll help you."

But before I could move to see her problem better, she stopped me with a protest.

"No, I can get it, and don't you dare laugh at me."

"I'm not laughing," I said, trying to look solemn.

Just then her ankles came loose and she swung off the berth in one motion, hit the deck, and stalked off to the bathroom. *Mad as a wet hen*, I thought, *but cute.*

We bought those ankle bracelets from a street vendor a few days before in Madurai, a large city in southern India. We went there to see the huge Hindu temple that covered an area of about fifteen acres in the center of the city. Steep stone roofs marked each of the twelve entries, of which two were ten stories high. Stone carvings of people, Gods, animals, and decorations in a myriad of poses, designs, and colors covered every square inch of each roof. For a few rupees, a self-proclaimed guide took us to the roof of an adjacent store to see the riotous, motley of colorful stone carvings up close.

Visitors; Indian and foreigners alike, milled about inside the temple. Worshipers sat at the feet of statues of their favorite gods. Hundreds of candles permeated the air with the scent of burning wax. The semi-dark interior looked surreal with contorted figures carved on stone walls, unusual geometric designs painted in bright colors on the ceilings and walls, and baroque-like figures carved into stone beams and columns. But most awesome for me was a disembodied deep bass voice humming a mantra of two notes over and over and over. It never stopped, and the sound formed a backdrop almost lost in the noise and confusion of the temple. No matter where I went, that ubiquitous low drone pulsated through the air, seeming to come out of nowhere, almost like imagination.

After leaving the temple, an Indian woman sidled up to us holding out several silvery metal bangles for us to look at. Each bangle consisted of loose interwoven chain link supporting silvery beads that dangled loosely in disarray.

Doris thought they were pretty, and asked, "What are they?"

Without answering the woman swooped down to the sidewalk and fastened one around Doris's ankle.

"Oh, look," said Doris, "it's an ankle bracelet. I've seen a lot of the Indian ladies wearing these."

Then she lifted her foot off the ground to see it better, and shook it to hear the jingle of the metal bracelet.

"Do you want it?" I asked.

"Oh no. I don't need this."

"For heaven's sake, if you like it, get it."

"Well, if you think it's okay?"

This was a typical conversation before Doris ever bought something for herself.

"How much?" I asked the vendor.

We agreed on a price that seemed reasonable to me, comparable to the cost of costume jewelry at home. So, I hauled out some rupees to pay her.

"Wait," she exclaimed raising her hand palm out in protest. "Are you not this lady's husband?"

"Yes," I replied, puzzled.

"Ah, then you need a second bracelet."

With that she swooped down again and placed a bracelet on Doris' other ankle.

Then she went on, "Married women wear two. A woman wearing just one signifies that she is available."

Available? I thought, while Doris giggled. *Good grief.*

"I think we were victims of a scam," I told Doris later. "That saleswoman probably made up the story about the meaning of two bracelets just to get us to buy another."

"Would you like me to test your theory," asked Doris sweetly. "I can wear just one."

I never brought the subject up again, but it turned out that she couldn't get either of them off anyway. Try as she might she couldn't figure out the clasp arrangement, and refused my offer of help.

"It's okay," she said, "I'll just wear them to bed."

She had been wearing them now for several days and was no closer to solving the problem of getting them off. I thought it was kind of humorous, but didn't dare laugh.

Shortly after that purchase, we were walking down a street where noisy people, crowds of them, took over from noisy vehicles after sundown. Everyone seemed to come out in the evening to stroll about. I loved watching the Indian ladies in their bright colored saris, so graceful and beautiful. The night was balmy and the air felt deliciously cool after the day's heat. Vendors cooked Indian fast food in carts in the street or on the sidewalk. The smell of cooking meat, garlic, and onions clashed with the aromas of nutmeg, cloves, and other spices I couldn't recognize.

Two girls passed from behind and kept looking back

over their shoulders at us. *Lordy, they're pretty,* I thought. I felt flattered they seemed so obviously smitten. Suddenly, one of them came running back to us and threw her arms around Doris's neck. Not my neck. *Rats.*

"I love you," she said to Doris.

That was all, and she ran ahead to continue walking with her friend where they quickly disappeared in the crowd.

"Why did she do that," I asked, feeling just a little slighted.

"I don't know. Do you suppose it's these ankle bracelets?"

"Well, if it is, I'm going to buy a pair for myself," I replied.

Doris, back from the toilet room, interrupted my reverie, and I helped her up to the top berth. Then, I slept a little while until daylight, when the people in our compartment woke and got ready to face the day. Women combed and braided their long black hair, while the men shaved using battery-powered shavers. The strong scent of aftershave lotion suddenly blossomed in the stuffy air of the compartment. Then came the disgusting noises of hawking and spitting, part of the normal Indian ritual of early morning, and the movement of people to and from the toilet room down the aisle at each end of the coach.

We got off the train at Sanchi to see the ancient Buddhist stupas located in a National Park. A two-tiered system for the purchase of entry tickets cost a few rupees, perhaps fifty cents, for Indian nationals and a whopping ten dollars each for foreigners. The ticket lady at the entrance told us that park fees had increased astronomically after Bill Clinton visited India; he thought the National Park fees were too low and recommended that they be increased. The result was fees so high that most budget travelers no longer visited the park.

We decided the fee was exorbitant for us, too. Instead of visiting the park, we hired a tuk-tuk, a motorized rickshaw, to take us to the nearby caves at Udaigiri. No fees. There, we had a choice of twenty Hindu and Jain cave shrines to visit that were hand carved out of the sandstone cliffs between 300 AD and 600 AD. I thought the best of all of them was a Jain cave at the top of a small hill. We entered through the roof of the cave and went down a steep flight of steps into cool twilight. The cave had a few rooms lit by windows cut through the wall, and we enjoyed great views out over the countryside.

We met an Indian family there and sat on carved rock benches with the parents a few minutes while the children continued their noisy exploration of the cave. The Indian woman told me that the nearby statue of a seated man was Buddha, but I knew it was from Jainism. He did look similar to a slimmer version of Buddha, but the background decorations and symbols proclaimed Jainism. Besides, my guidebook told me that eighteen of the caves here were Hindu and the other two were Jain. No Buddhist temple. Her error didn't surprise me, because most Indians are Hindu and know their own Gods better than Buddha. But after stating my conviction once, I let the subject drop.

At one point the Indian woman looked down at Doris' ankle bracelets and asked, "Are you from India?"

"Oh no," replied Doris, smiling. "I'm from the United States."

"I didn't think you were from our country, but we do have many different people here. Your skin is brown and you wear ankle bracelets, and I thought you might be from a remote area somewhere."

"I'm flattered you think I might be an Indian lady," said Doris.

"Well, of course, you can't be an Indian woman without wearing arm bracelets."

Then she took off half a dozen of her many bracelets and insisted that Doris slip them over her hand onto her arm.

"There," she said, "that's much better."

Outside the cave they hugged each other before parting.

On our last train ride in India, headed for New Delhi and our plane ride home, we were alone in the compartment with a young contemporary Indian woman. She cut her jet black hair short and wore Western style clothes. We had been talking quite a while when she mentioned Doris's ankle bracelets.

"I wear one too," she said, moving her foot to make her bracelet jingle. "They go with modern dress or a Sari, don't you think? Some day I may wear two if I ever marry."

"I like them," said Doris, "but I haven't been able get them off. I can't figure out how the clasp works."

"I'll show you," said the young woman, and Doris moved to sit beside her. Doris brought one foot up on the seat and the young woman flicked the bracelet off in a quick move with one hand.

Doris laughed and said, "You'll have to do that again, slower."

Doris learned the intricacies of fastening and unfastening ankle bracelets. And like their sisters the world over, they laughed and chatted intimately, while I sat silently watching them from my seat across the aisle.

At Play Among Scary Animals: Botswana

Scary animals aren't just those that would like to eat me up. I knew that in some areas in Africa, camping out in the open simply made me a piece of meat lying about, a potential meal for a hungry beast. But almost every animal I hoped to see, including those that didn't eat meat, out-matched me with their horns, teeth, claws, speed, and strength.

Starting on a camping and walking safari into the Okavanga Delta, a game park in Botswana should have been a time for sobering thoughts of potential dangers. Instead, in heady excitement, Doris and I helped the other six adventurers and the guides load up six boats with tents, camping equipment, food, and water for a three day outing. The guides included six men who maneuvered the boats through the water with long poles, a cook, and the chief guide-in-charge.

The boats, called mokuros, looked similar to a canoe with a flat bottom and no seats. They carried two passengers, their gear, and the poler, who stood at the rear and propelled the boat forward by pushing his pole against the bottom of the marsh. Once, the local people carved mokuros from a single tree trunk, but environmental education had come to Botswana. Now, factories mass-produced them, using plastic. The new mokuros were no longer quaint, rustic, or romantic, but they saved a lot of trees, and outlasted the former wooden boats by many years.

The delta was an unusual place where a whole big river, the Okavanga, disappeared in the middle of the Kalahari Desert. But before it completely disappeared, its waters formed a giant marsh with numerous islands scattered throughout. We planned to camp and walkabout, looking for animals on one of those islands.

We poled, single file, through shallow water choked with vegetation, mostly reeds and lily pads, leaving behind a narrow watery track through the lush greenery. None of it grew high enough above the water to provide shade, and the sun beat down on us mercilessly. At first, I sat upright in the bottom of the boat with my legs straight out in front of me craning and twisting to see everything I could. I saw very little except swishing reeds beside me, and the next mokuro ahead. Soon, my back and legs ached so badly, I had to change to a more relaxed position, reclining on my pack, like Doris in front of me, had done already.

Floating across patches of open water was a welcome change from parting our way through thick reeds. I saw the other boats against the background of large vistas of dark green vegetation contrasted against a beautiful, deep blue sky. The boats glided slowly along on brilliant, glistening waters that reflected the intense heat and light from the midday sun. I felt like a fillet lying on aluminum foil in a blue and green broiler. We passed a few islands, betrayed by their tantalizing, shade-producing trees towering above the reeds, but their shadows never reached us.

The guide, standing erect, saw far more than we did and enjoyed any scrap of moving air above the suffocating vegetation, but clients were not allowed to stand in a tippy mokuro. The edge of the boat extended about three inches above the water, and every so often refreshing drops of water sprinkled my face from movement of the guide's pole pushing us through the water.

Doris lay with her fingers idly splashing the cool water, and I warned her. "Don't dangle your hands in the water; they say it's like trolling for crocodiles using hands as bait."

"How can a crocodile swim through water, choked with so much vegetation?" she asked. "Are you sure any of them are around?"

Soon after, we both saw crocodiles lying on a mud bank, when we passed close to their island. Several waddled to the water's edge and slipped silently into the water to disappear below its surface.

"I guess that answers my question," said Doris, as she moved her body slightly so that nothing projected over the edge of the boat.

I had already done the same thing. No sense in letting a hungry crocodile get the idea for a quick swim-by snack.

We came across several groups of submerged hippos

when in open water. Most of their huge bodies floated underwater with only their ears, eyes, and nostrils showing. The guides tried to stay away from them. Instead, they crept around the hippos poling through the lily pads close to the edges of the brushy vegetation and reeds. Every so often, several hippos raised their heads, opened wide their huge jaws, showing off immense molars, and bellowed out a deep bass chorus in a deafening concert. I loved it when they did that.

"They're so cute," exclaimed Doris.

"Yeah, cute like a tank and easily provoked. I read somewhere, that hippos kill more people than any other animal in Africa."

"Yuk," said Doris, "you won't see me swimming in these waters."

"Not so much by swimming. People get trampled when they get between a hippo and water. I don't think it's on purpose, though. People just happen to be in the way when the hippo makes a mad dash for the safety of his water hole."

"But they look so funny when they yawn like that."

"I don't think they're yawning. I've been told it's a sign of anger and aggression. They could easily chomp our mokuro into pieces, and if that didn't get us, the crocodiles would."

"I still think they're cute," said Doris, in classic discount of everything I'd just related.

Before landing on the island of our intended camp, I heard loud splashing noises. The guide stopped poling, and I sat-up straight, eager to see what caused the commotion.

While we waited, a herd of elephants came in sight, a primeval mass of grey might including massive adults with huge tusks, juveniles, and babies. They churned the waters frothy as they waded in front of us inexorably headed for the same island. *Maybe we should consider another island,* I thought, but we continued poling toward shore in their wake. *Maybe the elephants cleared out any crocodiles hanging around.*

We unloaded the mokuros, and the chief guide assigned us spots to set up the tents. He spaced the tents at least fifteen feet apart in the theory that if elephants chose to go through our camp they would have room to walk between the tents. I thought the theory was flawed. Whether an elephant stepped on a tent or not was simply a matter of luck.

That afternoon, Doris and another member of the group went with a guide on a walking safari across the island. Too tired to go, and almost comatose from the heat, I lay about in the deepest shade I could find. When they got back we heard their stories of watching the herd of elephants up close. So the next morning, we all prepared to go on a walking safari.

We started out late, because the cook didn't get breakfast ready on time. Up before dawn, he saw a pair of red eyes next to one of the tents watching him. He went back to bed rather than face an unknown menace alone in the dark. In daylight we found the tracks of the "red eyes," which the guides identified as a cape buffalo. He had tramped among the tents for awhile and then left.

"These look like cow tracks," said Doris.

"Yeah, I guess they do. But this guy's got massive

horns and a bad temper. He'd just as soon charge you as look at you."

"Great, he's charging around our island somewhere, and we're going out for a little walk to see him?"

"You're darned right I'd like to see him," I said. "He's one of the five most prestigious animals in Africa that everyone wants to see on safari. The others are lion, leopard, elephant, and rhino. The big five," and I held up five fingers.

Walking along on the lookout for big game we saw sables, gazelles, zebras, and lots of warthogs. When they saw us the warthogs scattered away in all directions running for dear life. After their bodies disappeared in the tall grass, we still followed their movements by watching the tip of their tails held rigidly erect, just visible above the grass, as they zigzagged madly away from us

"They are really funny when they run like that," said Doris, laughing.

"Yeah, but not so funny if they don't run, and you're faced with a couple mean looking curved tusks, sharp as a razor."

"I suppose so, but those warts make their faces so ugly, they're cute."

Warthogs are cute? Doris thought all animals were cute, and she had a collection of stuffed ones at home, all named, of course.

In our wanderings we came to an open grassy area where we found a lone cape buffalo peacefully grazing.

"Is that the one from camp?" asked Doris.

"No way to know," I said, " they all look alike to me."

He was standing near a large termite hill which was

ten feet high and looked more like a two-foot diameter cylindrical tower than a hill. The guide got us organized to close-in on the buffalo using the termite hill as a screen. When we finally got there, we crouched around its base, peeking out on either side of the tower at the buffalo who was about thirty feet away. His head was upturned as he started at our hiding spot, still munching the grass in his mouth in a sideways motion of his jaws.

He was a big male with massive horns that formed a cap on top of his head before spreading down and out, and then curving up to end in points. They looked so heavy I thought he might have chronic headaches, which would account for his notoriously cranky behavior. His neck had a permanent downward bend, maybe from the weight of those horns, so he couldn't bring his head up above his shoulder. To look up and around, he tipped his head back while his neck stayed bowed, which gave him a baleful, malevolent look. I gave up my vantage point to someone else for few minutes and when I got to see him again he was closer to the termite hill, staring straight at our hiding place and pawing at the ground.

"He don't see too good or hear too good" whispered the guide, "but he can smell us good."

With that, we backed off trying to keep out of the buffalo's line of sight by keeping the termite's two-foot tower between us and him.

"If he charged us now, the termite hill will stop him won't it?" asked Doris.

The guide didn't answer, but gave her a little crooked smile with a slight shake of his head.

"Are all you men crazy?" Doris hissed at me. "Why do you have to see every stupid animal up so close?"

Later on a sandy beach, the guide pointed out the imprint of wrinkled skin where several elephants had rested. They had lain with their heads propped uphill, to make it easier for them to get to their feet faster. We saw their footprints, and the guide pointed out that the front feet leave "O" shaped prints and back feet leave "U" shaped prints. He said a lot of other things, too, that I immediately forgot. I fidgeted and watched Doris stifle a yawn knowing we both preferred to see and do things on our own rather than listen to a guide ramble on about stuff that was of no interest to us.

Finally, the guide found us a lone elephant, a huge male. One at a time we crept up close to look at him, hiding under heavy brush, just like our ancestors probably did a thousand years before. When my turn came to peek out at him, I saw a great gray body about fifty feet away rolling about on its back in a mud hole. The creature's huge legs flopped about in the air in an uncoordinated, upside-down dance. To me, the scene was so comical I laughed to myself.

Just then, someone behind me pushed forward a little too hastily and snapped off a branch of the bush hiding me. Suddenly, the great gray blob materialized into one helluva big elephant. With dazzling speed, he was on his feet facing my hiding spot which I now thought was pretty inadequate to hide anything. He raised his trunk with a high-pitched scream. Giant ears extended from his body at right angles making him appear as big as a house. I wasn't laughing or even smiling when he took a couple of menacing steps in my direction. The guide got us out of there fast and kept looking back over his shoulder to see if that juggernaut followed us. A thought came to me too late. *Where could I go? Where could I hide on this island if an elephant decided to come after me?*

I remembered a lecture on the correct things to do if confronted by a threatening animal. I had to stand motionless for some, climb a tree for some, and run like hell from all the others. But I couldn't remember for which animal I should do what. I guess my tendency would be to run and hope that someone in the party was slower than me. At seventy four, that looked less and less likely.

Technically, we didn't run away from that elephant, but we had a good incentive to walk very fast. I quickly ran out of breath and stumbled along panting like a steam engine.

"Are you okay?" asked Doris in a low voice, knowing I had heart problems.

"Yeah, but I feel like we're climbing a big mountain," I gasped.

"You've got to stop and rest," she said, in a concerned voice. "Just stop right now and the rest of the group will, too."

Doris worried about me a lot. I didn't stop, but I slowed way down, and we got a little behind the others. Finally, the group did stop their non-running running away. My heart got a chance to catch up on its duties of pumping blood to all those little wimpy cells inside me, crying out for more oxygen. I thought of it as a mechanical problem, and as a former engineer, I knew that some day practical heart pumps would be available to me, if I could just live long enough and survive stuff like running away from elephants.

Later that afternoon, the group crammed into two mokuros, and the guides poled us through the marsh interspersed with open waters to a swimming hole, a place free of reeds and other vegetation. Other than a patch of open water, I don't know what criteria determined a place safe enough to swim with the hippos and crocodiles. Doris and I opted out and stood on a piece of squishy land, on the lookout for crocs or hippos lunging out of the water with gaping jaws full of healthy teeth. The youngsters with us, in their thirties, played and splashed about unconcerned, as if at home on a local beach. On the way back to camp, the sun set in a red sky reflected on the water. Ribbons and patches of reds, pinks, and gold shimmered between the reeds, now dark green, almost black, as the light failed.

Later, back at camp, Doris looked around at the nylon tents, now appearing less colorful and cheerful in the fading light.

"How can these skimpy little tents protect us at night from the wild animals?" she asked. "I mean, what keeps them from simply tearing the tents apart?"

Too late, I thought. *Too late to be worrying about that, now.*

"I don't know why," I said, "but no animal has ever been reported damaging a tent on purpose. They never go after the goodies inside, although I bet they can smell us."

"You're telling me it never happens?" she asked.

"No. I'm telling you it's never been reported."

"Great, if you're eaten-up, you can't report it, right?"

"Hey, don't worry. We've got a lot of guides here and a good fire going. Nothing bad is going to happen."

That night after supper, Doris and I made one last trip to the toilet our guides had dug earlier, simply a hole in the ground a little way from camp. Neither of us wanted to leave the tent in the middle of the night to go stumbling about in the dark facing the unknown while looking for a hole in the ground. The chief guide had insisted we use only that one place for a bathroom, something to do with not attracting unwanted varmints, while in camp.

True to the guides' predictions, the hippos came ashore after dark and started munching on the grass. They were a noisy bunch, grunting like giant pigs and bellowing throughout the night. They sounded very close and I kept expecting one of them to squash our tent. Not on purpose, of course.

Later on, just before dozing off to sleep, we heard a loud snap of a tree limb broken off right behind our tent and heard it crash to the ground next to us.

"What's that?" whispered Doris, clutching my arm.

"It's our friend, the elephant, out having a snack."

"Well, I sure hope he doesn't come through our camp," said Doris, hanging on to my arm with an iron grip. "I don't think anyone told him about the fifteen-foot rule."

"Oh, I don't know. Maybe they tried, but couldn't speak his language."

Doris supervises the loading of a mokuro.

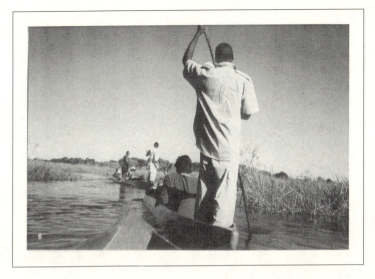

Poling through marshes on the Okavango Delta.

A Road Trip without Roads: Paraguay & Bolivia

"Not again," I muttered to Doris.

Our bus had stopped behind a line of busses and trucks, mostly oil trucks. The driver stepped out of our bus to investigate the problem ahead and came back shaking his head. He waved his arms and spoke something incomprehensible. Because of our meager Spanish and the other passengers' meager English, we were always the last to know the news. Finally, after several questions and pantomimes back and forth, we learned that two big oil trucks were stuck in a large mud hole, blocking the road with no way around them.

"Another delay," I said, "but then, that's nothing new on this road trip."

"Don't get so upset," said Doris. "We're on vacation. There's no place you have to be."

"Oh yeah? We only got ten more days to go, and if we keep getting stopped like this, we might have to miss something I want to see."

"Face it," said Doris, "you're just not going to get to

see and do everything in your lifetime. You're going to have to miss a few things. So slow down and relax."

I knew Doris was right. Someone else had told me those same thing years ago. Yet, I never stopped trying. I still wanted to do and see everything. But now, I think I was more surprised than annoyed that we had stopped again, because I thought we had left the worst of the road behind us when we crossed into Bolivia. Back there, the single track we had followed through the wilds of Western Paraguay was so bad it was almost nonexistent.

We had left Asuncion early in the evening and just beyond the city ran into a heavy rain. Five hours later, torrential rains still pelted the bus as we rode through the countryside in utter blackness. The driver finally stopped and parked for the night near the Mennonite settlement of Filadelfia, where the paved road ended.

"I'm not getting off this bus for anything," I told Doris as I tried to see out of water-streaked windows.

"What if you have to go to the bathroom?" she asked.

I didn't answer, because I didn't know.

By daylight, the rain had stopped, leaving behind a land completely covered with water, not a dry place in sight. The biblical flood came to mind. I did what everyone else on the bus was doing and went back to sleep. Later, I awoke to see land poking out of the water, here and there. I noted with relief that our bus was now on a piece of relatively dry land, and we could leave it to go to the bathroom without getting wet. Muddy maybe, but not wet.

In the black night, I hadn't seen the grimy little store/

café/hotel next to us, so Doris and I, along with other passengers got off to explore. The toilet room outback had a door of sorts that we couldn't close. Water gushed from the base of the toilet when flushed, and much to Doris' annoyance, it had no seat. We had long ago given up assuming toilet rooms in South America would have toilet paper, and we carried a good supply wherever we went.

The establishment had a few windowless cubicles that passed for hotel rooms that made our bus seats look luxurious by comparison. After one glance in the dark and dirty kitchen, I refused to eat there. The store had plenty of warm bottled water, beer, and Coca-Cola. A few canned and packaged foods, covered in dust, lay stranded here and there in clumps on the numerous, mostly empty shelves. Not much there to pique the appetite. But in one corner I found a treasure, a little crate of fresh tomatoes sitting all by itself. I bought the whole crate, thereby cornering the market on tomatoes in our new world, the bus.

To my disgust, the driver refused to budge until he thought the dirt roads ahead were dry enough. This left us sitting around most of the day in muggy heat close to 120 degrees. I sat in the shade moving as little as possible, hoping for a breeze to cool me off. Not noted for my patience, I complained to Doris about our wimpy driver. At least, if he went on, we would have a little breeze from the movement of the bus.

"Relax," said Doris, who was somehow having fun communicating with the other passengers, although she knew even less Spanish than me. "Didn't you want to have some adventure on this trip? Another night on the bus won't hurt us. We slept okay in our seats last night."

As usual, Doris saw the brighter side of any discomfort we encountered and kept my spirits up. On our travels, I initiated most of the fun adventures which she would never think of doing. But once on the way, she cheerfully supported them which allowed me to think of even more adventures to try.

The driver finally decided to go late in the afternoon which was the start of another twenty-four hour period on our journey to Santa Cruz in Bolivia. The road was much more saturated than I thought it would be, and we went through several mud wallows longer than the bus and wheel deep. The driver gunned his way through them, and we skidded and bounced with sickening lurches through the mud. I kept wondering what would happen if we got stuck or ran off the road. Fortunately, the surrounding land was flat, and I didn't think we could get badly hurt if the bus hurled us off the road. But how would we get back to civilization?

"Will you give me a piggyback ride if we get stuck in the mud?" I asked Doris in jest.

Her hands clutched the armrest, and with her face set in deep concentration, she mentally drove that bus through one more mud hole. She didn't say anything, but I doubt amusement was on her mind.

That evening, bouncing around on the bus, we feasted on crackers and cheese, dried fruit and nuts from our packs—and, yes, fresh tomatoes. Though not our favorite drink, we shared some warm beer smuggled aboard the bus by other passengers. It was available only in one-liter bottles, but I liked the novelty of that, and one bottle was more than enough for Doris and me.

The road got progressively worse, and the mud road became a sand road. A road in name only. It consisted of two tire tracks rutted a foot deep in the sand. In some places the tracks disappeared in a confusion of churned-up sand where vehicles obviously had trouble passing each other. I kept reminding myself that this was the main road, the Trans-Chaco Highway, and the only land crossing on the 400-mile border between Paraguay and Bolivia. At nine o'clock that evening, the bus jerked to a stop, stuck in the sand.

"Everyone out," ordered the driver.

Of course Doris and I didn't understand him, but we watched in amazement as all the passengers trooped off the bus.

"Come on Doris, we've got to go. The driver wants us off the bus."

In the pitch black of night, men and women strained to push the bus free of the sand as the driver revved the engine and gnashed gears to jerk the bus forward and back. Finally, it broke loose from the sand to go roaring and careening up the track, stopping a quarter of a mile away to reload the passengers.

Back on board, everyone began to talk and laugh about the experience. A little further on the bus got stuck again. We got off and pushed again. The first two or three times were somewhat of a lark, lots of talk and laughter. But this went on until 3:30 a.m.—six and a half hours!

No more talking and laughing, now. No more larking, just a grim job.

After my second effort at pushing the bus out of the sand, I stood leaning over, my hands on my knees, panting like a steam engine with my heart revved-up to its maximum. In the light of several flashlights, a knot of curious passengers stood watching me. So when I finally caught my breath and stood erect, I explained.
"Mi Corazon es muy mal." (My heart is very bad). That created quite a buzz and, when the driver found out, he banned me from pushing his bus another inch.

"Jeez, I don't want these people to think I'm a lazy shirker," I told Doris later.

"You're crazy," said Doris. "These people have more sense than you. They have enough problems, and don't need some macho foreigner having a heart attack trying to push a bus, for God's sake."

She said a lot of other things too, and I got the message.

When off the bus, an inky blackness surrounded us except for the brilliant stars above. Not one single manmade light could I see except for the bus. . The only thing tying us to civilization was the primitive track we followed, and the thought of being left behind alone in that dark expanse was disturbing. *How would we get back if the bus left us out here?*

Doris and I grew tired of slogging through loose sand, and our return to the bus got slower and slower. I blamed it on our age at seventy-one-years-old, but Doris thought we were simply out of shape. At one point Doris realized that all the other passengers had disappeared, walking back to the bus faster than we could. We were stumbling along alone in a black void, trying to catch up to the bus. Way ahead, we saw the beam of headlights radiating from a seemingly invisible bus. The lights appeared to be dancing in the night air.

Doris let out an ear splitting yell, "Stop. Wait for us."

"They can't hear you," I said.

"They'll forget us and leave us behind," she cried out to me.

"Not likely," I said. "How many gray-haired gringos are there on that bus? Only two," I quipped. "So we'd be pretty hard to miss."

"But the lights are still moving," she said, still very agitated.

"Those headlights aren't going forward so the bus must be waiting. Besides, a lot of the other passengers couldn't have made it back to the bus yet."

We finally arrived at the sanctuary of our bus, the last to get aboard. Some of the passengers smiled and clapped, rejoicing with us, I assumed.

"We thought you had left us," Doris said, out of breath.

The driver smiled, shook his head, and pointed to our two empty seats.

At last the bus remained unstuck. I kept waiting for it to get stuck again, but it kept grinding along through the sand. No one spoke. No one cheered. And in that calm quietness, I fell into an exhausted sleep.

In the morning, we passed the frontier into Bolivia,

coming to the main North/South arterial. Although unpaved, the dirt road carried heavy traffic with all of the buses and oil trucks heading to and from Argentina. But we saw no cars. Elated, I thought we had made it. The worst was over. With input from the other passengers, I figured the drive to Santa Cruz might take another ten hours or so. We optimists figured we would be there that day by late afternoon or maybe early evening. We were partly right in that we arrived in late afternoon, but on the following day. Here we sat, stopped again. This time by two oil trucks stuck in a mud hole blocking our way.

By the time I understood the problem, the driver was already backing up the bus to get to the small village of Gutierrez which we had passed earlier. Since he couldn't turn around on the narrow road, he backed up for about five miles to the edge of the village where he could turn to drive the bus forward again. We traveled backward very slowly as the engine labored and whined in reverse gear. I thought I could walk about as fast as the bus backed down the road.

We parked for the night in front of a little store that faced the plaza. To Doris's delight the building next to it housed a spotlessly clean bathroom with flush toilets, sinks, mirrors, toilet seats—the whole works. The owner charged fifty pesos to pee, and his fee went up from there. He had one problem though, no running water. So, he hired teenagers to haul in water in five-gallon cans which they dumped into 55-gallon drums set just inside the door. He supplied plenty of buckets for his clients to dip into the barrels for water to flush and wash hands.

"Aren't we lucky?" asked Doris, "to have a bathroom so close to our bedroom?"

To her, the bus had already become a bedroom for the night. Along with the rest of us, she expressed dismay when the owner locked up the bathroom at 7:00 p.m. and went home for the night. He didn't open again until 7:00 a.m.

The village was too small to support a restaurant, and the fast food prepared in the little booths along one side of the plaza looked inedible. So that night we fed on crackers, tomatoes, canned beer, and a small piece of fried chicken traded for one of our tomatoes. The beer from the store was good and cold, going down easily with our meal.

By now, many of the passengers were like one big family, although some remained aloof the whole trip.

One of the first friends Doris made was with a woman from Asuncion, named Rita. She was about thirty years old, talkative and brassy. We liked her, and many of the other passengers did, too. She talked to us a lot, but knew as few words of English as we knew of Spanish. We took the time to listen carefully to each other, trying hard to communicate. And got pretty good at it. In addition, she had big breasts. Those attributes attracted the driver as well as some of the other male passengers. The driver was a small, lithe man in his early forties who talked easily with the passengers and wore a lopsided grin most of the time. He invited Rita to sit in front with him in the seat normally reserved for the assistant driver. She never refused the offer, and changed seats with the assistant quite often. She engaged the driver in long, intense conversations, and I could only hope that he eyed the road as much as he did her breasts.

The cab had a jump seat between the driver and Rita, and she would, with the drivers consent, occasionally invite other people upfront to sit with them. Such was the power of a well-endowed figure. I made it upfront once, but Rita invited Doris several times. They were the best and most exciting seats in the house,—an ideal place to see mud holes, or trucks rushing head-on toward the bus.

But now, we sat in the parked bus after supper in that sleepy little village working on some crossword puzzles to pass the time until we were tired enough to go to sleep in our seats sitting upright again. Idly, I noticed a bus cruising around the plaza picking up people. Three passengers from our bus jumped ship and climbed on with them. I learned they were going on that night in order to reach Santa Cruz by morning. As quickly as I could, I arranged to meet that bus in a few minutes for us to go with it, too.

"Are you sure you want to change buses?" asked Doris. "I trust our driver to get us through. He might take a little longer, but I'm sure we'll get there safely."

"Come on Doris, we can be in Santa Cruz by morning. Get your stuff together. We've got to hurry because they won't wait."

Doris trusted my judgment most of the time, and hardly ever mutinied. So we hopped off our bus and headed across the plaza to meet the bus that was leaving, but it had already gone.

"They didn't wait," I wailed.

"It's just as well they didn't," said Doris, sounding a little relieved.

As it turned out, she was right. We were lucky it left without us.

Later in the evening, Rita asked us to join an impromptu mini-fiesta with five of her buddies from the bus. I felt flattered to be included in such an exclusive group, but it was mostly because they liked Doris.

Our little group of merrymakers stood at the edge of the street in back of the bus, talking, laughing, and drinking ice-cold beer. We passed a couple of cans of beer around, and each person took a sip or two before passing it on. When gone, one of us bought another couple cans to pass around. We talked in Spanish—very little English, but lots of pantomime and laughter, which everyone understood.

The village had no such thing as trash barrels; so, we went native and tossed our empty beer cans in the dirt street where, over time, I suppose they disappeared into the mud. This was difficult for me to do since every nerve ending in my body cried out against littering.

At some point, Rita set the cans upright in the road to form a pyramid. Each of us got two chances to knock over the cans with a stone, and the person leaving the most cans upright had to buy the next round. Doris and I managed to knock over enough cans to keep from buying more beer, but the biggest man in the group missed all the cans with two mighty throws. He bought more beers with good grace while enduring good-natured taunts and laughter from the others. The fun and laughter continued until the flow of beer dried-up, when the lady selling it closed her store for the night. Still weary from my workout the night before, or perhaps because of all those little sips of beer, I went right to sleep. I went out like a light, sitting upright in my seat for the third night aboard our hotel on wheels.

I awoke when the driver started the engine at 5:30 a.m. He drove around the plaza honking the horn to gather-up those passengers who had wrangled beds in private homes for the night. He appeared determined to get started early and probably woke the whole village in his mad rush to get on the road. Dozens of trucks and buses had stopped in the village for the night. They cluttered the streets, haphazardly parked, making driving about the village difficult. By the third time around the plaza, we had picked-up all the missing passengers and were on our way.

We arrived at the place where we had turned back the day before. The road sloped into and out of a thirty-foot depression, and at the bottom was a slough about the length of three buses. The two trucks stuck there the day before had mysteriously disappeared. The driver ordered all of us off the bus, "Consigue por favor del autobus." By now I easily understood those words: please get off the bus. With the others, Doris and I made our way around the edge of the muddy water. At the bottom, we gave up trying to find dry ground, and sloshed through the water getting our feet and ankles wet in the process. Doris hated to get wet.

"Darn, I'm getting soaked," she sputtered, obviously exaggerating.

"Hey, you're not going to melt. Only witches do that."

"But I'm all wet!" she fumed. "What am I going to do?"

"Just wait a few minutes, and I bet you'll dry out."

Doris ignored my attempts at humor and sat on a rock, grimly pulling her shoes off to dump a small stream of water out of each. I always wore sandals, which never collected water—sand and gravel maybe, but never water.

Partway up the slope beyond the mud pond, I stopped to watch the bus come through. The driver backed up to the top of the small rise to gain maximum momentum. Then, he suddenly gunned the engine and the bus leaped forward, charging down the slope straight for the water. It hit with a mighty splash, and muddy water parted in front of the bus like the bow wave of a boat. Water flew high in the air covering the entire bus in a muddy film. It lost velocity quickly, and for a few seconds I thought it might be floating with no wheels touching the ground. The momentum carried it to our side of the pond, the tires grabbed, and the bus lurched up out of the water to grind up the hill past me and the other passengers to wait at the top to board.

Everyone gave the driver loud praises, and I grinned and gave him a thumbs-up as I passed by on the way to my seat. My estimation of his determination and driving skill had just gone up several notches.

"I think we're going to make it," I said to Doris when I sat down.

"I knew we would," she said. "Rita says she travels this road a lot and always goes with this same driver, because he's so good."

"I guess he must be good," I said, thinking Rita's persuasive figure could entice any driver she wanted.

"No matter what it takes, he's determined to get us to Santa Cruz, even if there's a worse disaster ahead."

Her words were prophetic A little after noon we stopped once more behind a long line of buses and trucks parked on the side of the road.

"Good grief," I said, "we've only got two more hours or so to get to Santa Cruz. What now?"

I got out with the rest of the passengers and counted ten parked buses before I came to the problem. The mother of all quagmires, about half the size of a football field, obliterated any sign of a road. Churned-up mud and standing water filled the entire area. Around the edges, watching the unfolding drama were hundreds of people.

"Where did all these people come from?" asked Doris.

"I don't know, unless there's a town across the way. We didn't pass one on this side."

Then it hit me.

"Wait, these must be the passengers from all the parked and stuck buses. If each one holds forty people, ten of them would provide a crowd of four hundred. And I'm sure there are more buses than that."

Four buses were stuck in the quagmire in various positions. Two Bolivian army bulldozers were at work One churned through the mud pulling a bus for a short distance until the bus tilted to one side, threatening to overturn. The second dozer, hooked to another bus, pulled until it too listed dangerously, ready to roll on its side. That dozer stopped, and several men wading in knee-deep muck swarmed around the bus working with the dozer trying to get it upright again.

"Look over there," said Doris, pointing to one of the stuck buses. "See, it's the one that left last night. Remember the one you wanted to take? Aren't you glad we didn't get on? It looks permanently stuck in the mud."

"I can't remember the exact bus," I said. "Are you sure?"

"Well, it's the same bus I saw, and it's mired in muck right before your eyes."

"I didn't see it very well in the dark last night," I muttered, hoping she would drop the subject.

But Doris doesn't like to drop subjects when she knows she's right, and went on. "Just think, if we had gone with that bus last night we might be still stuck here tomorrow. Honestly, I'm sick of sleeping on a bus and eating fresh tomatoes."

"Well, we're not through this mess, yet," I replied.

Fortunately, one of the bulldozers chugged and rattled its way to a point near where we stood and began working on a bypass around the quagmire. We turned away from stuck buses to watch the new action. It began dozing a primitive track through the brush and small trees, and our driver, seeing this, went back up the road and drove his bus to be first in line behind the working dozer. A line of buses and trucks quickly formed in back of our bus, and my assessment of the driver went up yet another notch.

We passengers walked along the primitive track as each vehicle ground its way through the makeshift detour. The dozer pulled each vehicle through a short section of mud and water where the outlet flowed from the mess on the main road. Our driver had to get down in the mud to connect the tow cable from the dozer. By the time we caught up to our bus on the dry road beyond the quagmire, the driver was standing next to it, barefoot, with his pants rolled up to his knees. Splattered mud coated him from head to toe in a terrible mess, but his bus stood ready to roll. We all cheered and, with a flourish, he gave us a little bow.

Two hours later we arrived at the bus station in Santa Cruz. Friends and relatives of the other passengers had been waiting for almost three days. A road trip scheduled for twenty-four hours ended up taking sixty-eight hours. We said our farewells and received hugs from our new friends of three days. By the time we bought onward bus tickets for the following day and returned to the platform, everyone had left. Except for a very muddy bus, it was as if nothing unusual had ever happened, just another routine road trip in South America.

Passengers survey their buses stuck in the mother of all mud holes.

Bus listing on a sea of mud.

Bringing in the Hay: Switzerland

"Let's do it," said Doris.

"Do what?" I mumbled around a mouthful of food.

"Didn't you hear the hostel warden asking for volunteers to bring in the hay tomorrow?"

"Is that what she was talking about?" I asked, knocking back the rest of my beer I had with supper.

"You never listen." said Doris, not for the first time in our short life together. "She said rain was coming, and the farmers need help getting the cut-hay off the ground and stored before it gets wet."

"Oh, I heard that, but I didn't think she was talking to us."

"She was talking to all of us," said Doris with a little exasperation creeping into her voice. "And I think we should go help out tomorrow."

Doris tries to help all creatures great and small. I try to stay out of it, especially when dealing with the four-legged kind that are bigger than me.

We were eating supper in the crowded dining room of

The Mountain Hostel in Gimmelwald, Switzerland. That hamlet's only connection to the world and grocery stores was via a cable car or a forty-minute walk through alpine meadows and stunted fir trees to the village of Murren, which was a larger village connected by a rail system and cable cars to the hubbub of life in the valley way below.

The Mountain Hostel, formerly known as a Youth Hostel, changed its name when older people, like us, started to rent their beds for the night. Young people with their enormous packs filled the hostel to capacity. Our packs were minuscule by comparison. Looking around at the laughing, cheerful faces sitting at our table and sharing the same long benches, I figured we could be the grandparents of many of them,—and certainly old enough to be parents of the rest. Despite our age differences we felt right at home, and Doris gossiped non-stop with several of them.

I sat silent and relaxed, recovering from the battle of the kitchen. I had cooked our dinner amid at least ten other would-be cooks in a space only a little bigger than our kitchen at home. Shortly after we met, Doris and I had come to an amicable arrangement. I cooked the dinners and she cleaned up. We each got our own breakfast and lunch.

The kitchen had two electric stoves much in demand because some of the young cooks needed two, maybe even three burners for their dinners. Noting the problem of only eight burners available, I chose to cook my famous one-pot dinner consisting of cut-up meat and vegetables made edible with a spicy sauce. I had to fight to get my one burner and stand guard while the meal cooked. If I turned away too long, I found my pot shoved to one side to make way for someone else's dinner.

Just cutting up veggies was a challenge while elbowing other cooks for a little counter space. We stole each other's knives shamelessly. Leaving a bowl, utensil, cutting board, or any such items unguarded for a few seconds meant its loss to a temporary owner. In this ongoing melee, only the strongest and fittest survived.

After supper, we signed up at the front desk to go haying in the morning before wandering off toward bed. The single men and women slept decorously in separate dorms, yet the only bathroom was open at all times to both sexes. Thank goodness for solid doors on toilet stalls and showers. The bed in each dorm room was simply a wall-to-wall communal platform accessed by a narrow aisle at the foot of the platform. Hostel rules required that all packs and personal gear be stored in the sleeping rooms which made each room a crowded mess and hard for anyone to move around.

"Which rooms are messier, men or women?" I asked Doris, the expert on dirt and mess.

"I couldn't tell," she said, wrinkling up her nose as if smelling a bad odor.

"According to the warden, there are seventy-four people staying at this hostel.

"No wonder it's so cluttered," she said. "I don't know how they can cram so many people into such a small place."

In the room set aside for couples, though not necessarily married, Doris and I shared a bunk bed.

Doris always liked the top bunk, which was okay with me because I could get out of the lower bunk easier to go to the bathroom at night. The two-tiered beds jammed the room so tightly with aisles so narrow I had to be careful not to hit someone in the next bunk with a flailing arm when turning over. Doris was a neat freak, and had a hard time dealing with packs, gear, and castoff clothes strewn about our bunk. Several times, I had to restrain her from tidying-up other people's stuff. I spent a lot of time awake that night listening to coughs, groans, and the furtive noises of boys and girls at play.

The farmer's wife, Rosemary, met us at the entrance of the hostel early the next morning with a small flatbed cart hauled by a tractor. She had an older woman with her and three young children. Five of us who had signed up for gathering hay jumped aboard the cart for a ride to work.

A bright sun shone in a cloudless sky with no sign of rain, and I asked Doris, "Do you think this is a scam to get some cheap labor?"

"Hush," she said in a low voice. "Just enjoy the experience in this beautiful place."

She was right, of course. We were amid an alpine setting straight out of a Walt Disney movie. The site for the hostel was spectacular. Snow covered mountains and bright green meadows surrounded us on all sides. Mountaintops glistened in their snowy white mantel, which contrasted sharply with dark gray cliffs and rocky crags thrusting out of the snowfields and glaciers. Below the snow and rock, large areas of desolate loose scree lay on steep slopes, giving way to pastel greens of the upper alpine meadows which in turn fell away into the dark green forests that splashed-up the side of each mountain from their sources in the deep valleys below. Here and there, for contrast, ribbons of white water cascaded down from the snowline to disappear in the trees far below.

Across the valley stood the massive peaks of the Eiger, Monch, and Jungfrau, so close and clear I thought maybe, if I tried hard enough, I could reach out and touch them. I noted with satisfaction, that the monk still stood guard between the monster and the young maiden, as he had since those peaks were first named.

The farmer's field lay above Gimmelwald on a steep patch of ground lying downhill from the road, where grass lay drying in the sun after being cut by hand. When we got there, Rosemary's husband, Petra, and her father, Walter, were already raking hay. Walter, white-haired and close to my age, showed me how to rake the grass downhill into piles. He watched me as I took over his rake, and then stopped me for not doing it right. *What's right or wrong about raking?*

"No, no," said Walter, "rake all the grass. Leave nothing behind. If you don't do it right, my neighbors think we're sloppy wasteful farmers."

I looked at the meager wisps of grass left behind, and they reminded me of the relentless war Doris waged against dirt that, most of the time, I couldn't see. From then on, I carefully raked-up every scrap of grass, whether I could see it or not.

At lunchtime, Rosemary called us up to the road where she and her mother served fresh crusty bread, homemade cheese and sausage, and spiced tea. We sat at the edge of the road, eating and drinking-in the sight of the mountains across the way. I just couldn't get enough of them. I wished I could be right there on the glaciers in their midst.

"Still not a cloud in the sky," I said, looking around. "No rain today."

"It doesn't matter," said Doris. "We get credit for doing a good deed whether it rains or not."

After lunch, we continued to form piles of hay while Petra and Walter winched them up to the road with ropes and a large tarp. There, they fed loose hay with a pitchfork into a compactor that stuffed it into a trailer enclosed with woven wire. When full, Petra hauled the trailer down the road to his barn, unloaded it, and came back for more. We finished raking just before they winched the last pile of hay up to the road.

Rosemary offered everyone a ride down to the village on her cart, but Doris and I opted to walk back. We wanted to savor the rest of the day alone and soak up the intoxicating views of the mountains around us. They soon left us behind and passed out of sight. When we finally came to the village, we stopped at Rosemary's house to buy her homemade cheese to take with us in Doris's little daypack which I was growing more and more thankful she carried.

Like others in Gimmelwald, Rosemary decorated her house with long boxes at every windowsill filled with bright colored flowers. She invited us into her house through the lower floor that served as a barn for animals such as goats, sheep, and horses. The animals were gone, probably out in pastures, but we smelled them and saw their straw bedding strewn about the floor. She led us up a stairway into the living area above the animal pens and on into her kitchen. Rosemary stored her cheeses in a special curing room off the kitchen. Two or three-dozen wheels of cheese, four inches thick and twelve inches in diameter, lay aging on shelves across two walls. The rest of the room contained vats, a table, and cheese-making equipment. Rosemary picked out a wheel with a hunk already cut out of it, and with a large knife, cut-off a sizable wedge for us.

Back at the hostel, the warden greeted us cheerily. "It's supposed to rain tomorrow. Thank you for bringing in the hay."

Then she gave us each a free token for a shower.

Doris turned to me and said, "There, aren't you glad you did it? Where else could you get a free shower for a day's work in paradise, while doing a good deed?"

Doris loads hay.

I learn to rake hay.

Guatemala through a Side Door

My worst travel nightmare had come to life. Doris and I were stuck in a tiny remote village with no place to stay overnight—No hotels, no rooms to let, nothing. I had voiced this fear several times to Doris in our travels, but she had always simply shrugged it off.

"Someday, traveling the way we do, we might find ourselves sleeping on a park bench," I had said.

"We can always do better than that," she had replied. "Quit worrying."

Until now, we had always managed, one way or another, to dodge that bullet, and never got to sleep on a park bench. Looking around at what I saw of Bethel, Guatemala, I was pretty sure this village had no park, much less, benches of any kind.

We had crossed the frontier from Mexico by small boat, and landed in this forlorn place carved from the jungle. Pigs and chickens ran loose, rooting or pecking in the dirt and garbage. Here and there, ditches drained to the river carrying slimy-looking water with the odor of an outhouse. A few piles of rotting garbage sat waiting for a garbage truck that I figured would never come.

Hampered by my poor grasp of Spanish, I asked a lot of questions before learning that we had missed the noon bus out, and the next one came at 6:00 a.m. the following morning. My stomach lurched to rock bottom as I realized we had no choice but to stay the night in this dismal place. My next series of questions brought us to the only available place to sleep the village offered. Our so-called sleeping quarters were adjacent to a house that served food to the public. But I wouldn't want to eat there if they did. Close enough to the river people threw their garbage toward the water, but a lot of it never got that far. Garbage and debris littered the area down to the edge of the river.

The place the villagers showed us had no windows and a door that wouldn't latch. Some light and ventilation entered through cracks in the wood plank walls and we had a peak-a-boo view of garbage and the river beyond. The only furnishings consisted of a bare mattress lying all by itself on a dirty floor. I think someone threw it in the room just before we got there. We saw suspicious stains from former users and it smelled of mold and other things. I shuddered at the thought of the creepy crawlies lurking just out of sight getting ready to come out at night and play. No ceiling or netting provided a barrier from the thatched roof, a haven for spiders and other bugs to drop in on us if we were dumb enough to sleep there.

"This isn't a room," said Doris, "it's stable with a mattress in it. Look, you can still see straw in the corners."

"I don't think they have horses here," I said. "Pigs, chickens, goats maybe, but not horses. Do I take it that you're turning down this fine room?"

"You can sleep here if you want," she said, wrinkling up her nose, "but I'm going to look for a park bench."

We had started from Palenque, Mexico, early that morning expecting to get to Flores, Guatemala, by late afternoon. Palenque was the site of extensive Mayan ruins and the jumping-off point to get to Guatemala via the Usumacinta River which formed the border of Mexico and Guatemala. The minivan from Palenque dropped us off in the village of Frontera Corozal where the road ended at the river. There, the driver turned the minivan around for the return trip. We were the only tourists, and he assured us that he would take us back if we wished.

"Yo espereme aqui diez minutes," he said. "I wait here ten minutes."

After looking around at the tiny, primitive village of Frontera Corozal, I wondered how many people took him up on his offer. We hooked up with a boatman who agreed to take us up river to the village of Bethel on the Guatemalan side of the river. The Usumacinta River, about three hundred-feet wide, flowed between steep mud banks past the two villages on its way to the Gulf of Mexico, over two-hundred miles to the north. He guided us to the frontier office of customs and immigration where we got our passports stamped out of Mexico.

As we started down the mud bank to the river, Doris whispered to me, "I need to go to the bathroom before we get on that boat."

"Why didn't you go at the customs office?" I asked.

"I thought I could wait, and besides, I didn't want to ask that grumpy-looking government man."

Once again Doris's bladder took control of the trip. Our guide, the boatman, understood the problem and went looking for a toilet room. After a few minutes, he found a woman willing to let Doris use her family outhouse for a few pesos, though no toilet paper, of course. That pit stop led us to a grubby little store that sold, among other things, candy, pop, and peanuts. Since we were going into Guatemala, we used-up the last of our Mexican pesos and bought peanuts.

Then we walked and skidded down the bank to the river. The boatman pointed out one of several similar-appearing boats tied to the bank and we boarded it. He called it a *lancha. Close enough to a launch*, I thought. It was about thirty-feet long and seated six to eight people facing each other at mid-ship. We were the only passengers and sat across from each other sheltered under an arched roof of thatch. We had a fun ride up-river through a couple minor rapids and past large boulders sticking out of the water.

After traveling about an hour on the river, we landed on the Guatemalan side, a few kilometers down-river from our destination at Bethel. The boatman urged us to get out of the boat and follow him up a trail from the water's edge through thick jungle. We soon lost sight of him because we walked too slowly. In a very short time the jungle hid the river from our sight and soon after we lost the comforting sounds of its swishing, gurgling, and splashing waters. I felt alone and cut off from the world I knew.

"Where are we going?" asked Doris.

"I don't know, but as long as we stay on this trail we can get back to the river."

"But what if the boatman's left us?"

"I don't think he'd do that. We haven't paid him yet."

"I know," said Doris, "but what if he doesn't come back?"

"We'll go back to the river and hitch a ride on another boat."

"That could be a long wait. I didn't see one single boat on the way here."

Puzzled and uneasy by the boatman's behavior, we continued to follow the trail through dense foliage, dappled in shadow and bright sunlight. We heard the raucous cries of birds and saw their bright bits of color as they flitted through the trees. From everywhere came the sounds of insects, buzzing and clicking, while some chirped like giant crickets. Rotting vegetation permeated the air with a rank earthy smell. Suddenly, we heard loud roaring from an animal close by in the jungle. I nearly jumped out of my skin, and I felt prickles of alarm on the back of my neck.

"What's that?" yelped Doris as she clutched my arm. "Do they have tigers here or something? It can't be a lion, can it?"

By that time I had recovered and knew what it was.

"They don't have tigers and lions here," I said, "just jaguars."

"A jaguar?" she squeaked. "Let's get out of here." And she started to turn around to run back to the river.

"No, wait. I didn't say that roaring was a jaguar; it's howler monkeys. They sound terrible, but as far as I know they're not dangerous."

Just then another chorus of roaring erupted from the jungle, and Doris jumped, but she stood her ground and didn't run.

"A monkey?" she asked in disbelief. "How can a monkey make such a loud noise?"

"I don't know, but if you listen carefully, it's not just one. There's several of them. I guess they just open their throats and let her rip," I said with a half smile on my face.

"You heard this before?" she asked.

"The first time I heard it, I was sleeping out in the jungle in a hammock and almost peed in my pants. I thought for sure I was about to be eaten."

Now that we knew what caused the noise, we tried to enjoy it as part of the jungle experience. Each time we heard them roaring we stopped to listen. The troop of howler monkeys traveled away from us and their roaring became fainter until finally we couldn't hear it anymore.

We came to a park-like grassy clearing and heard the boatman talking to someone off to our right. Ahead of us was a large wood building, with no walls open under a conical thatched roof. Before we got any closer to the building the boatman came back explaining that this was Pasada Maya, a place to stay overnight.

"It's closed," he said shrugging his shoulders with his

hands palm up. "The manager is gone, and his wife says it's closed."

"It's okay," I said. We're going on to Flores anyway, and don't plan to stay here tonight."

He shook his head once, but didn't say anything else.

On the way back to the launch, Doris asked me in a low voice, "Why did he stop his boat to show us a place to stay?"

"I don't know," I answered.

But now, standing on a dirt street in Bethel with no place to stay, it hit me that the boatman knew more than we did. He knew we couldn't make it to Flores this day and we would have to stay overnight. He had just been trying to help us out.

I asked more questions and somebody finally pointed the way to the immigration office where we went to get our passports stamped into Guatemala. A desk in one corner of the office served as the bus terminal and the clerk there assured us that a bus came at 6:00 a.m. followed by another at noon. The ticket lady was sorry we missed the noon bus, but suggested we could stay out at Pasada Maya, and she flung her arm out and pointed in its general direction.

"It's very close," she said. "Only three kilometers," and she held up three fingers in the European style: thumb, first, and second fingers. "You can walk there easily from here."

"It's closed." I said. "Our boat stopped on the way here, and no one was there."

"His wife was," said Doris, "and she said it was closed."

The ticket lady seemed surprised to hear that news and said she would ask a cousin of the owner about it when she saw him. We went next door to an open-air café with a thatched roof set within three-foot high walls and sat at one of their picnic tables to order a late lunch.

"Okay Doris, we have about sixteen hours to go before that bus gets here at six in the morning. This looks like a pretty good place to hole-up and wait it out."

"What are we going to do for sixteen hours?"

"We can read through the afternoon," I replied, "or walk around a little, eat a leisurely supper tonight, and then flake-out right here on a picnic table."

"You don't think the ticket lady will get any good news about Pasada Maya?"

"It's possible," I said, "but we should get prepared for the worst."

"Oh well, this isn't so bad," said Doris, looking around. "At least we have a roof over our heads, and the pigs can't get in."

"Yeah, and look at all the choices we have for beds."

The lady running the café looked a little surprised at our request to stay the night, but she had no objection. We had solved our dilemma of finding a safe, clean place to sleep.

Later that afternoon, a well-dressed man speaking excellent English arrived at our café/hotel. *Where could he have come from in this forlorn village?* He told us that Pasada Maya was open, and that we would be very welcome to stay there. He was sorry for the misunderstanding.

"Are you sure?" I asked, not wanting to risk hiking to a place only to find it closed.

"Beyond a doubt it is open," he said. "I guarantee it."

Whoa, I thought, *that sounds like an owner talking, and a very smooth one, too.*

We packed up our stuff, headed back to the river, and turned right at the stable we had refused earlier. Beyond the last house in the village floodwaters had washed out the narrow dirt road in two places, but its remnants led us on through the jungle to finally end its existence at Pasada Maya. The river was somewhere off to our left but we never heard or saw it. One of the older boys of the village accompanied us, walking his bicycle beside us saying he wanted to practice his English. But I thought the suave, well-dressed man who came to us at the cafe probably sent him along just to make sure we got delivered to the right place.

We met the manager, David, and his wife, Elena, waiting for us at the main building. It was a round, open-air structure, raised about four feet off the ground, and covered by a tall conical thatched roof. The use of natural tree-trunks for exposed rafters and beams made the interior appear rustic and inviting. Its area was large enough for one long table down the center of the circle seating ten people on each side. A small enclosed kitchen/office sat discreetly to one side attached to the rim of the dining room.

David spoke some English, perhaps a little less than my Spanish, Elena spoke no English. Even with the help of our guide, whose English turned out to be pretty basic, understanding each other took a lot of effort.

They had rooms available for the night. Something was wrong with the generator, though, so they couldn't cook dinner for us in the kitchen.

"Do you still want to stay?" asked David.

"Let's look at the room," said Doris.

Neither of us expected too much out here in the middle of nowhere, but we were willing to take a look. After all, it wouldn't take much to beat a picnic table. Lack of a cooked dinner was not a problem. We always carried a few goodies in our pack to snack on just in case.

Elena accompanied us to the rooms—six thatched huts arranged in an arc a few hundred feet away and out of sight of the dining room. The clearing ended right in back of the huts and the jungle pressed in to form a mottled backdrop of confusing shapes and patterns in monochromatic shades of green. The colors of natural wood and thatch of the huts contrasted, but also complemented the vivid greens of the jungle.

"This is so beautiful," said Doris.

"Incredible," I said. "It looks like we're in the middle of some romantic movie set in the jungle. All that's needed is a smooching couple."

"I'm available," said Doris, as she came over and pecked me on the lips.

Elena showed us the bathroom first, a separate structure sited to service all the huts. What a surprise to find clean sinks, toilets, and showers—all with running water. I didn't press my luck to ask about hot water.

Our hut had a lock on the door, windows with screens, and solid walls with no peek-a-boo holes. The management even furnished us with candles and a mosquito coil laid out on the nightstand between the beds. The top of the stand was clean natural wood, devoid of food stains, watermarks, or cigarette burns which was the norm at many places we stayed.

"This place is neat and clean," said Doris. "Very homey."

"Better than neat," I said. "This place is upscale. It even has screening over the interior surface of the thatch to keep bugs out of our space, and in the thatch where they belong. I don't think we've ever had this luxury before."

"Yes," I said to Elena, smiling and nodding, and we all went back to the dining room

Walking back, I said, "There's no way we can make that six o'clock bus out of here in the morning."

"Who cares?" said Doris. "This is fun, and there's always other buses."

Back at the dining room our guide with his bike was still there talking to David even though daylight was fading fast. Doris and I sat at the table and brought out some rolls, crackers, tangerines, and the Mexican peanuts. We sat in the semi-dark under the thatch watching as the daylight outside faded away. Elena excused herself to go home to start dinner for her family while some light still remained. We offered some peanuts to the guide who promptly plunked himself down as if to stay for rest of the evening. David brought out a lighted candle and set it on the table in front of us. The surrounding twilight made the light of that one candle appear festive.

"I have beer," David said suddenly, "but it's not cold."

Wow, I thought. *Where did that come from? The road's washed out. Maybe by boat?*

I wasn't much of a beer drinker, but out here with nothing else around and trying to make a meal from dry rolls and crackers, it sounded delicious.

"We'll each take a beer," I said without consulting Doris. "And bring one for yourself and our guide," I went on, while pointing at each of them, and pantomiming drinking.

They got the picture and soon the four of us sat at one end of the table sipping beer and eating peanuts. The meal became a feast, and the little candle appeared even more festive.

Doris made a face after a sip or two of beer, and said. "Too bad we can't put an ice cube in it; this stuff is horrible when it's warm."

"Hielo," exclaimed the manager. "Ice, I have plenty. It is cooking we can't do. Do you want a bowl of ice?"

"Yes," Doris and I exclaimed together.

"Wow. Where did the ice come from?" I asked. "Out here without electricity?"

I never got an answer but, like magic, the manager returned with a large bowl filled with pieces and flakes, obviously chipped from a big solid block of ice. What a wonderful transition the ice made from warm to cold beer.

Finally, our friendly guide with his bike left for home. By now, the night was black as pitch, and I wondered how he could see the road back to the village more than a mile away. *He must have eyes like a cat*, I thought. David wanted to go home too, but not before bringing us two more beers before leaving. Doris and I sat in silence; alone, enjoying the peaceful night beside our cozy candlelight. Beyond our cone of friendly light, a lonely, unknown blackness surrounded us, and I was reluctant to leave.

When we finally decided to turn in, I took the candle to light our way, shielding it with my other hand to keep the flame from flickering out. Its light parted the darkness in front of us as we made our way to our little haven in the jungle.

Just before going in for the night, I blew out my candle and asked Doris to stand beside me facing out toward the clearing. We had already lit the candle in our room and its light shone weakly through the window behind us. When our eyes adjusted to the dark we saw hundreds of fireflies pulsating their ethereal light into a black void. Coming and going, never still, they left tantalizing, minuscule trails of light in the darkness before winking out.

"This is enchanting," I said.

"It's beautiful," said Doris. "What a wonderful day this has been."

"Incredible," I said, as we stood close with arms around each other.

I was very happy to be here sharing this moment with Doris, but I felt a little uneasy being so alone in such a strange place.

Then, out of nowhere came the roaring of a troop of howler monkeys destroying that peaceful moment.

I shivered as we both turned to go inside. I locked the door and felt safer. In bed, I left the candle burning a little longer until familiarity with our room made our little world inside feel snug and safe. After blowing out the candle, I lay awake in the dark listening to the calls and shrieks of night birds, the furtive rustling of small animals, and the everlasting background of buzzing, chirping, and scritch-scratching noises from insects. The howler monkeys kept moving away slowly through the treetops and I tracked their progress as their howling became fainter. I think Doris was almost asleep when she said in a small voice, "I hear a men's choir out there, like in a church. It's such beautiful singing."

"There's no church choir out there," I said. "It's the howler monkeys."

I don't think she heard me, though, because just before her deep breathing told me she was asleep, she murmured words that just weren't in her normal vocabulary.

"Incredible…Enchanting…"

A feast in the jungle by candlelight.

Upscale sleeping accommodations amid the jungle.

A Zipper among the Roses: Czech Republic

Disaster struck me in a public restroom just five minutes before our tour started. I had finished using the urinal and like hundreds of times before, reached down to zip up. Only this time the zipper wouldn't zip all the way. It was stuck partway up. I tried moving it back down to start over but it remained stuck at half-mast.

Frantically, I messed with it trying to jerk it loose, muttering curses under my breath. Other customers who came and went going about their business looked at me a little strangely. I tried to peer down at the zipper to see what was holding it stuck but the angle, or maybe my protruding stomach, kept me from seeing much. Now, the other men were really looking at me. I was far more interesting than a normal trip to the urinal.

I had to leave this place, open zipper or not. Doris and I were at the palace of Hluboka Nad Vitavou, near the city of Ceske Budejovice. We had purchased tickets for a guided tour of the castle and it was about to start. Doris was waiting, which was not a good thing to let go on too long. So I took off my sweater, draped it over my arm, and held it to cover the front of my trousers. Now, no one would know. Then I walked nonchalantly out of the sanctuary of that restroom to meet Doris and face the knot of strangers waiting for the tour to start. I swear they all looked at my sweater and smirked.

"What took you so long?" asked Doris.

Funny, that's normally a question I asked her.

"Come on," she said, "the tour is about to start. Why are you holding your sweater in such a funny way?"

"Because I can't get my blasted zipper to close," I responded in a low voice.

"Oh, I see. It's kind of like a screen. Good idea," she whispered with a big grin.

"This is not a laughing matter," I sputtered.

"I'm not laughing," she said trying to look solemn.

"I can't go poking around the castle like this," I said. "I've got to go back to the restroom and fix this dad-blasted zipper."

"Oh, come on. You're fine. No one can see, and I sure won't tell anyone. When we're done with the tour, I'll fix it for you."

"How are you going to fix it, without I take my pants off?" I fumed.

"Don't worry, I can fix it. I'm an expert at zippers. Come on, the tour's starting," she said as she grabbed my arm and pulled me along with the others on tour.

The castle was an endless blur of ornate rooms with carved wooden ceilings, each room filled with large beautiful furniture. My arm got tired of holding the sweater awkwardly in front of my lower belly. Sometimes I forgot or the sweater came unraveled, and I'd turn to face a wall scrutinizing a piece of artwork while readjusting the sweater and resting my arm. I lagged behind the others a lot, thinking I would be less conspicuous, but maybe that theory didn't work. I'm sure I caught several whispers and significant looks in my direction.

Finally, the tour ended at a gift shop, of course. I hustled Doris out of there as quickly as I could which was hard to do since she had a great affinity for gift shops. But, at last, we were in the clear. Out in the open. The rest of the tour was self-guided along walkways that meandered through open woodland and manicured lawns. Most of the tourists didn't bother walking around the grounds and went home but we opted to go off by ourselves to fix a zipper.

Doris bent over in front of me and started fooling with the zipper while I stood lookout for anyone coming down the path. Suddenly, a short distance ahead, a couple turned onto our path from a side trail that I hadn't seen and there we were; caught, with Doris peering intently at my crotch and fussing with my zipper. I don't know what those people thought about seeing two gray-haired, sixty-eight year olds in such a compromising position. I gave Doris a late warning and she popped upright in time to smile and return their subdued greeting. Without smiling back, they hurried past us down the path.

By now, I had had enough.

"Give me your scissors," I yelled to Doris, "and I'll cut the blasted thing out."

"Don't be silly," she said. "That won't help."

"Yes it will," I fumed. "At least I could pee again if I had to go. Right now, I don't even know if I could get these stupid pants off with the zipper stuck part way up."

"Come with me over behind those rose bushes," she said, pointing to some skimpy roses a little way off the path. "You can watch for anybody coming, and I'll stay hidden from their sight."

"How can you hide behind a rose bush, for crying out loud?"

"You just stand there. They'll see you, but won't even notice me. Besides, maybe no one will come along."

But of course, a whole clump of people came along chattering and laughing. They saw me and got very quiet. A few waved but we were too far away for gentle greetings and I nonchalantly waved back. Most of them walked on but I noticed one or two stop and look at me again before hurrying on to catch up to their friends. At last Doris got the zipper to work and stood up.

"There," she said, patting me several times on the closed zipper. "It's all fixed."

"Cut that out," I yelped, "somebody's liable to come along."

"Oh my, aren't we sensitive?"

" Come on, Doris. Those last people saw you; I know they did."

"No, they saw you, and were fascinated by what they thought you were doing."

"What do you mean?"

"Anyone who saw your A-frame stance would know immediately that you were peeing on the roses."

"I was not."

"I know, but how could they tell when you were so well hidden behind these roses."

"But, but—" I sputtered before going silent.

How can I argue with such logic? Oh well, it's not like we'll ever see those people again; and besides, Doris did fix the zipper and saved my pants from certain destruction.

Riding the Rails in India

"You want to do what?" cried Doris, with a little panic in her voice."

"Ride the trains in India," I replied gaily. "Just for a couple months, you'll love it."

I had already gotten her agreement to go to India, but only for two weeks. With some friends, we had signed-up for a two-week guided tour in Northern India, flitting around in air-conditioned buses and staying at five-star hotels. Now that I had that first inch I was asking for the mile.

She expressed her doubts.

"I don't think I want to travel a long time in India," she said. "It sounds like a dangerous place and I wouldn't want to go off alone, either. It's dirty. The people are so poor, and there's so much disease. I don't think it would be any fun traveling there."

"Of course it's safe. I wouldn't travel in a dangerous place," I replied. "We'll get our shots from the travel doctor and that should take care of any bad bugs."

"That means we'd be away from home for two-and-a-half months. I don't know how I can be away for so long. I'd rather not go."

"But we're already going," I said. "We would simply

extend the time a little. And just when have you ever had a bad time on one of these trips?"

I said a lot of other things too so she knew that I really wanted to go to India for a more extended time.

She was silent a minute or two, but I knew the trip was on when she continued in a reflective voice, "I'll have to stop the mail. The plants will need watering. I'd need to clean the house before we go."

Clean the house? Good grief, we won't even be here, but if that's what it takes to convince Doris to go—that'll be fine with me.

Fortunately, Doris and I loved to travel by train and preferred them to buses. We'd ridden the rails a little in Mexico and South America and had gone many places in Europe by train. Now we were tackling the fourth largest rail system in the world with thirty-six thousand miles of rail serviced by over 1.6 million employees. This made the Indian Railway the largest private employer in the world, as well as one of its biggest bureaucracies.

By the end of the cushy two-week guided tour, Doris and I were more than ready to jump off on our own. We hadn't seen much of the real India, just a veneer painted-over reality to impress and please the tourists. We had practically no contact with the Indian people other than liveried waiters and doormen in their flashy, corny uniforms. Our packs were already small by comparison to everyone else's on the tour but Doris and I pared them down even more. We left the excess stuff stored in our last New Delhi hotel to be picked up at the end of two months. Skipping the tour's farewell dinner we took the first train out of New Delhi and headed for the desert area in the state of Rajasthan with its forts, palaces, and camels.

Janet and Bruce, mountaineering friends of ours who were also on the guided tour, went with us for the first two weeks. Although first-class was available on some trains, we chose to ride second-class thinking it would be more fun and a better way to meet the everyday ordinary Indian people. Our procedure was to buy onward tickets and reserve a seat upon arriving at our destination, so we were always figuring out when to leave before we ever got to a place.

We tried to get window seats to watch the scenery roll by but, better yet, to control whether the window stayed open or not. For some reason Indians hated open windows, except when stopped in a station. Maybe our Seattle background made ventilation important to us, but without it, the coach became unbearably stuffy and hot. Whenever I got the chance I yanked the window wide open but usually had to settle with the other passengers for less opening than I wanted.

Each compartment was off to one side of the aisle and sat up to eight people during the day. From 9:00 p.m. to morning the seats converted to beds, reserved for six people on three tiered platforms on each side of the compartment. In addition, a bench facing the aisle made into two berths at night. So each compartment, although open to the aisle, was a cell containing a maximum of eight people, kind of like an extended family. People without reservations risked getting sent to an unreserved day coach, a place of bedlam, crowded with people and bundles.

At night, we lay on a bare padded surface using our packs for pillows. Usually, I slept like a baby, lulled by the swaying coach and the clicking of wheels on the track. Doris and I agreed that the top berth had the most room but its downside was the light that never went off and a rackety fan that never stopped turning. The bottom berth took second place with its potential for coolness and ventilation from the window. Neither of us liked the middle berth. We slept in our clothes but some Indian men changed to night clothes right there between the berths, modestly screening themselves with thin pieces of material the size of a small tablecloth. I asked Doris once if she ever peeked, but she gave me a stony look and didn't answer.

Many times after an all-night train ride, I awakened to the noise of the Indian men hawking, clearing their throats, and spitting out the phlegm. I didn't have the nerve to see where they spat. Doris told me later she covered her ears. But once this ritual was over and the men were fully clothed, they again became the courteous friendly people we knew from before, with no more spitting for the rest of the day.

We continued riding the trains after Janet and Bruce left us to go back home to Seattle. One morning at the end of an all-night trip, Doris and I walked down the platform toward the station to see about onward tickets.

"I have to go to the bathroom, really bad," exclaimed Doris.

"For heaven's sake, why didn't you go when we were on the train?"

"Because I didn't need to then," she replied.

"But," I sputtered, "that was just a few seconds ago."

"Well, I can't help it; I've got to go now."

This was a familiar conversation on our train trip throughout India. I finally learned to go with the flow, so as to speak, and we visited the ladies room in about every station in India. The toilet rooms on the trains did get pretty nasty by the end of a trip. They had a hole in the floor and, as the train swayed and jerked, it was a hard target to hit. If men didn't squat, they missed. Whatever the reason, Doris preferred the stationary holes in the floor of a train station. We found the ladies room and a short time later she returned, laughing.

"What's so funny?"

"When I went in, all the ladies were lined-up waiting in front of several stalls. But when I joined their line they smiled and motioned me to the next line. Finally, I ended up in the line farthest from the door."

"What the heck's going on?" I asked. "You have the right to wait in any darn line you want in a public restroom."

"Hold on, there's more," said Doris. "When I got in the last line they pointed to an alcove the size of a small bedroom. In the center was a Western toilet. Nothing else, just a toilet sitting all by itself, like a throne."

"No doors or anything?" I asked.

"No door, no curtain, no nothing. Just that ugly

white toilet sitting in the middle of the room," she said grinning.

"Oh boy, I would have waited right there in line to use the hole in the floor. At least those stalls have doors."

"I couldn't do that," said Doris. "Those Indian women were very nice, thinking of me. So considerate. And besides, at that point I had to go so bad. I didn't care."

"So, you used the toilet."

"You bet I did, but part way through my business, I looked up to see all the Indian ladies had left their lines and were peering in at me as if I were on stage. Then, when I brought out the toilet paper, they leaned forward and held their breath to see what was going to happen next."

"Just like the climax of a great play," I said. "So, what did you do?"

"What else could I do? I finished the performance and flushed the toilet. When I went out all the women were back in long lines, and they smiled and nodded their heads at me as if I had done something wonderful."

"Well, maybe you started a new fashion in toiletry," I said.

"I don't think so. Not one woman made a move toward that Western toilet, no matter how long their line was."

Traveling the trains during the day gave us more chance to talk with the other passengers. They were invariably courteous, and quietly sat watching us until Doris or I broke the ice by asking them questions. Many of the people we met spoke some English. Sometimes their curiosity about us was more than they could handle, and then they would initiate the conversation. Very few people other than Indians traveled by second-class coach, so we were generally an object of speculation.

One day, we began eating lunch after the others in the compartment broke out their food. After a few minutes, a man sitting opposite us abruptly asked a question.

"What are you doing?"

Surprised, it took me a second to realize he was speaking to me.

"We're eating," I said, my eyes wide open in puzzlement.

"Oh, please excuse me. What I wanted to know is why you put all your garbage back into your pack? No one here can understand why you do this," and he gestured with his hands to include everyone seated around us.

"Oh," I said, a little relieved. "We save our garbage to throw into a trash can whenever we find one."

"But—-" he shrugged and gestured to the open window where everyone else in the compartment had been throwing away their refuse.

"We don't like to litter," said Doris. "Besides, India is too beautiful to litter."

"But, have you not seen the mess we have here in India? The garbage you have kept is so little, it will not make a difference."

"Maybe, if everyone stopped littering, your mess would go away," said Doris.

The man across from us translated this to the others in the compartment before stating, "I am a teacher. And

I have decided to instruct my students with this idea of yours, that each individual can make a difference."

From then on, Doris and I noticed the other passengers packing away their garbage, and they threw nothing else out the window.

Later, I said, "Those people probably waited until we left the train, and then with pent-up relief threw their refuse out the window."

"You're so cynical," said Doris. "How do you know we haven't started an anti-littering movement that will sweep across India?"

Whenever the train stopped in a station the platform erupted in a frenzy of activity, color, and noise. Some women wore bright colored saris and others wore ankle-length pantaloons of a solid color with matching smocks down to their knees. All wore their black hair in one long pigtail, and they all liked to wear multiple bracelets on each arm. Many carried their wares on large trays and bowls balanced on their heads. The men dressed in western-style clothes that were far less colorful and interesting than the women.

Men and women swarmed past our open window, selling everything imaginable. Tooth brushes, jewelry, eyeglasses, pocketknives, articles of clothing, soap. Everything and anything, like a giant department store in motion. If we couldn't see the item we wanted, all we had to do was call out its name, and a few minutes later two or three entrepreneurs stood in front of the window offering that item for sale.

The vendors, men and women alike, did whatever

they could to get our attention. They yelled out the nature of the items for sale, elbowed each other for better position, waved and thrust their wares up to the window for closer inspection. Our window looked out upon a sea of organized chaos.

Occasionally smells of cooking meat wafted by the window making my mouth water, and spices permeated the air with exotic smells. Food vendors offered an endless variety of snacks and finger-food: deep fat-fried dough all puffed-up, light and crispy; samosas, filled with spicy vegetables; and dosas, stuffed with potatoes and onions spiced with curry, and served with fruit chutney. Then someone came by with iddly, little round rice cakes wrapped in newspaper, and served with a tangy, sweet/sour sauce in a plastic cup. Others offered fresh hot chapati served with a plastic dish of hot-spiced vegetables The food appeared in endless supply and variety, each dish coming by again and again. So, if I missed-out on the first round, the same kind of food came by the window again, if I simply waited long enough.

When finally tired of the confusion and noise outside our window, we sat in our seats in the relative calm and quiet of the compartment. In all that bedlam outside, new passengers pushed their way through and boarded the train. They brought a little of that noise and confusion with them as they found seats and settled in. At last, our compartment was full, and we sat quietly waiting for the train to depart.

A skinny, old woman entered the compartment to beg. She was tiny with a maze of wrinkles for a face. She made a beeline straight for us, holding out her little hand cupped for begging. This was something Doris and I were accustomed to in our travels. After all, they could tell we were strangers in their land and, therefore, must be very rich. I always felt guilty when I didn't give them something, and this time was no different. Doris and I had talked about giving to beggars. We wanted to help, but we had no formula of how or what to give. I felt a little better when all the other people in the compartment refused to give the old lady money.

"There, you see, we do have democracy in India," said the man sitting next to me. I must have looked a little confused, because he went on to say, "She has the right to beg, you see, but we, on the other hand, have the right to refuse."

I had never thought of begging in that way. I did have the right to refuse, and I didn't need to feel guilty.

"Do you ever give to beggars?" I asked.

"Oh, yes. I make it a point to give every day to someone I think is worthy. But only once during the day. In this way I hope to earn merits to help me achieve a better position in my next life."

From then on, whenever I encountered beggars overseas, I thought of that man's words on the democracy of begging. If I found someone worthy, I gave, but only once a day. And I never felt guilty again about refusing to give to a beggar.

Soon after the beggar lady left, I learned another lesson about Indian social life. A boy of maybe twelve years came into the compartment, and immediately began sweeping the floor on his hands and knees. He used a hand brush and a piece of cardboard for a dustpan. The people lifted their legs or shifted enough for him to sweep under and around the seats. When finished, he stood before each man in the compartment and, without words, every man, including me, gave him money.

"There, you see?" asked the man sitting next to me, "We are a capitalist country. We believe in rewarding enterprise and initiative. That boy provided us a service and has found a way to make some money without begging for it."

From then on, I realized that all those noisy Indian men clamoring to provide me with some useless service were actually entrepreneurs, and they did show a lot of initiative. They weren't beggars asking for money and giving nothing in return. Most of the time I really didn't need their services, but now, sometimes, I hired them anyway. It was my way of trying to help them gain some ground in a tough, capitalistic world.

One day, we were alone in a compartment when a family with three children came to sit with us. The mother wore a long, dark, robe-like cloak that extended from neck to ankles. A black cloth covered her face, so that only her eyes showed. Brownish-red tattoos covered her hands with intricate designs. Almost immediately the children came over to inspect Doris. In their eyes she was different from their mom, and they were uninhibited in expressing their pleasure and delight interacting with a smiling, cheerful Doris. The family spoke no

English and we didn't understand their language, but we communicated a little anyway.

At some point the lady felt comfortable enough to unfasten her veil, exposing her face to us. I could hardly believe my eyes as my jaw dropped, leaving my mouth open, because in all my travels I had never seen a woman unveil herself. What a pleasant surprise, because I had always wanted to see what lay behind one of those veils. She had a plain, pleasant face, but not particularly good-looking, and it destroyed my fantasies of seductive looking women behind those veils. Finally, the children got tired of Doris and went to play with their father and run about in the aisle.

The woman took Doris' hand in hers and gently stroked it with her fingertip tracing imaginary lines on it and up her arm. Then she pointed to her own decorated hands. Doris smiled and nodded. With that, the lady brought out her makeup kit and made designs on all the surfaces of Doris' hands and arms, using an almost clear liquid. Allowing that to dry, she mixed up henna and dyed Doris' hands and arms to the elbow. When finished, Doris had reddish-brown geometric designs and pictures of flowers and creeping vines all over both hands and arms.

Turning to the mom, Doris smiled and said, "Thank you, thank you so much."

It's my theory that "thank you" in any language, is understood by everyone. The mom nodded and broke into a large smile that suddenly, for a moment, made her look beautiful.

"Isn't this gorgeous?" Doris asked me, waving her reddish-brown arms in the air.

"Yes, it is," I said, wondering if Doris would still think it gorgeous when she couldn't wash it off.

When the train slowed for the next station, the family prepared to leave. Before fastening her veil, she and Doris hugged, and then the family left, leaving us alone in the compartment. It took a week before the designs faded and, by the end of two weeks, all traces of dye disappeared, leaving only the memory of that chance encounter.

The day finally arrived when we had to go home. But, Doris didn't want to leave.

"What's this?" I asked. "I had to practically drag you, screaming and kicking, to get you on the plane to come to India."

"No, you didn't," she said in an aggrieved voice. "I love India. It's beautiful, and the people are so wonderful; I'd come back in a minute."

Like many of us older people, Doris had a selective memory.

The Fiesta at Coixtlahuaca, Mexico

On Christmas Day, Doris and I went in search of a *fiesta*. Mexico had many festivals, and I supposed on any given day at least one celebration occurred somewhere in the country. However, I had a guide book which stated that the small village of Coixtlahuaca (Co-wheat-la-wa-ca) celebrated a *fiesta* the day after Christmas which included a parade, fireworks, and perhaps a rodeo. Not entirely trusting a guide book, I asked about the festival in Coixtlahuaca before we left Oaxaca. I got vague responses to my questions, but thought my meager Spanish caused confusion and misunderstanding. But then, maybe they never heard of that particular *fiesta* or the village either.

"Are you sure you want to go wandering off into the wilds of Mexico looking for a fiesta no one has ever heard of?" asked Doris. "That doesn't sound like a good idea to me."

"Just think of the fun and excitement," I said, "and we'll get to see fireworks and a parade."

"We could stay in Oaxaca and see that," she responded.

Doris was probably right. Oaxaca did have parades, somewhere in the city, almost every night, and promptly at midnight set off a few fireworks to end the evening. Oaxaca was awash with hundreds of people, like us, who had come to celebrate the Christmas season. Even more came to celebrate the Radish Festival, a national holiday held the day before Christmas Eve day, and lasting only for that one day.

Using radishes that looked a lot like big red parsnips, contestants carved them into intricate shapes depicting scenes of people, vehicles, animals, and structures. Everything and anything imaginable was carved from radishes. They fastened carved pieces together to make larger, more complicated items, such as carts pulled by burros, cut-away houses completely furnished, and a wonderful Ferris wheel. Each scene was displayed as an exhibit on a miniature stage, two feet by two feet set side by side and about four feet above the ground.

On the morning of the Radish Festival, judges examined the exhibits which extended around three sides of the plaza to determine which ones would receive prizes. Later in the afternoon, they unveiled the exhibits for public viewing, and by evening people jammed the plaza so tightly we could hardly walk around. I never saw so many people crammed into one place, all trying to view a bunch of radishes. Amazing. Many of them stood in a line one quarter mile long, for hours, waiting to view the exhibits up close on a controlled walkway built only that morning for that sole purpose.

Doris got talking to an American woman who had

been waiting in line for two hours. "Can we get you anything to eat?" asked Doris.

"No, but what I really need is a bathroom. Could you hold my place in line while I find one?" she asked.

When she got back, I asked, "Why are you doing this? Is it really worth waiting in line so long?"

"Probably not, but it's the thing to do at a Radish Festival."

Rather than wait in line to see carved radishes up close from a walkway, Doris and I settled for craning over the heads of people in line, or peeking between their bodies.

On the morning of Christmas Eve day, as if by magic, all the radishes were gone, and gone too were the exhibit stalls and walkways, as if none of it had ever existed. After Christmas Eve, the festivities quieted down, and people left Oaxaca in droves. No more parades, no more fireworks, and no more radishes.

The guidebook described Coixtlahuaca as a small village about ninety-eight miles North of Oaxaca—not far in distance, but certainly a long way from the hustle and bustle, noise and excitement of Oaxaca. An air-conditioned bus took us to Tamazulapan, the closest large town to our destination. On the way we passed the turnoff to Coixtlahuaca marked by a sign.

"Hey, that's where we need to get off," I exclaimed. " Darn, we passed the turnoff."

"Too late," said Doris with just a touch of elation in her voice.

"It's okay. We need to confirm our onward buses from

Tamazulapan anyway. Besides, we can probably catch a direct bus from there back to Coixtlahuaca.

At the bus station I asked about the *fiesta* in Coixtlahuaca. One woman nodded, smiled, and rattled off a volley of Spanish. I had high hopes until a little while later she left on an express bus to Oaxaca. She obviously thought I was asking about a *fiesta* there. Another lady I asked looked dubious and shook her head. Coixtlahuaca was still thirty miles away, over in the next valley. Maybe she had not heard of that village, or perhaps the *fiesta* was just not very popular.

"Should we give this up?" asked Doris. "No one seems to know anything about a festival."

"Let's not give up yet. I'm sure we can get to Coixtlahuaca, and we'll find out for sure about the *fiesta* when we get there."

I asked about buses to Coixtlahuaca and got the usual nods, a burst of Spanish, and vague hand signals which could mean that a lot of buses were going there, or none. Several buses stopped at the terminal, but none were going to Coixtlahuaca. I finally figured out that we needed to take one of the frequent buses going toward Oaxaca, get off at the turnoff to Coixtlahuaca, and hopefully get another bus to that village. My meager Spanish had failed me again, because I was sure that's what the local people at Tamazulapan had been trying to tell me all along.

We caught the next bus going in the right direction, and it dropped us off at the turnoff. The bus roared away in a cloud of diesel smoke and gnashing of gears, leaving us alone in the silence of a forlorn spot. A narrow gravel road led toward Coixtlahuaca. No bus waited there for us, no cars, no people, no nothing. We saw a couple small, derelict buildings across the main road, one advertising a beer, Dos Equis, in neon lights with the "E" winking on and off erratically. The surrounding area was a desert wasteland with scrub brush growing sparsely in the bare dirt and gravel. A slight breeze blew up small dust eddies that moved debris and plastic listlessly here and there across the littered ground.

"Neat place," said Doris, looking nervously around her. "What if there's no bus going to that village we want?" She still had trouble pronouncing "Coixtlahuaca."

"Well, if we can't get there, we'll just have to wait here until a bus comes the other way on the main road. It'll take us back to civilization and the Tamazulapan bus terminal."

"That dirty hellhole," said Doris. "Did you see their bathroom? No toilet paper, no toilet seat, and practically no water except what's running over the floor. Yuk. I'd rather go behind a bush and pee."

It wasn't that bad, I thought. *Maybe a little stinky, but otherwise okay.*

We waited uneasily at the edge of the road for something to happen. A passing vehicle, maybe, or people—anything to ease the silence and loneliness of that place. Suddenly, a vintage car came tearing down the main road and rattled to a stop beside us. In it were two male passengers, and a driver who assured us that this was a private taxi going to Coixtlahuaca. Doris looked a little dubious, and we hesitated. The driver jumped out and shook my hand while opening the back door. The passengers smiled, looked respectable, and nodded their assurances. So we got in for the short ride to Coixtlahuaca.

I asked about the *fiesta* there, tomorrow. The driver shook his head, and the passenger next to me smiled and said something enthusiastically in Spanish. *Definitely a mixed bag.*

"We should get out of here," Doris muttered to herself more than to me. Then definitely talking to me, she said, "No one seems to know what you're talking about."

"Well, maybe, but we'll find out for sure about the *fiesta* when we get there."

When we got to Coixtlahuaca, I lost a little confidence in the passenger sitting next to me when he didn't understand my Spanish for "hotel," which was the same in English: "hotel." The village of Coixtlahuaca consisted of one main street about six blocks long, with a few businesses and houses lining both sides, and a smaller parallel street with a school and government buildings. *Not a very big place to support a fiesta.*

Near the edge of the village stood a huge church with an even larger monastery attached. It was built in the mid-fifteen hundreds and was probably as much a fortress as a church at the time. Someone pointed us in the right direction, and we walked down the main street toward the hotel, and coincidentally, toward the church. We stopped on a corner and looked up at its immense walls and bell tower built on a level platform about ten feet above the street. The added elevation made the structure even more impressive, and easily seen for miles around.

Just then a band started to play. In Oaxaca that usually meant a float or a parade was about to pass, so I waited on the sidewalk in anticipation.

"Good, the *fiesta* is starting early," I said. "We don't have to wait for tomorrow."

"I'm not so sure," said Doris slowly. "There are no people around to watch."

Out from behind a retaining wall came some boys and a couple skinny dogs leading a band of six musicians. They played battered and dented instruments and looked just as scruffy as all the bands we had seen in Oaxaca. Then came men holding large lighted candles, and women carrying green fronds. And then, four men carried a casket followed by family and friends straggling along behind.

We found ourselves on an empty sidewalk, the only people in the whole village, watching a funeral procession. It came down from the church, turned, and passed by our corner. Embarrassed, I wanted to disappear into the walls of the building behind me. Everyone in the procession looked at us with curiosity. After all, we certainly weren't from that village.

"This is not the way to keep a low profile," I hissed.

We tried to travel unnoticed. I never wanted us to stand out, and we tried to blend in as much as we could with the people around us.

"Well, we can't run away." said Doris. "That would really freak them out."

The procession was small, and it quickly passed us by. My discomfort faded as we went on down the street toward the hotel.

Suddenly, high-toned bells in the church began to ring. Startled, I stopped to listen. Te-dum, Te-dum, they rang in a pure two-note pattern. A pause, and then again, Te-dum, Te-dum. Again a pause, then more Te-dums' in pairs. "Clear as a bell" came to mind. On and on, they rang without stopping until the procession reached the cemetery about a half-mile away in the valley below. Over the higher notes of the Te-dums, a large bell with a deep bass tone rang single notes: *Bong, Bong, Bong,* nine or ten times. After a pause of several seconds the lower-toned bell rang its single bass notes again. The bells were loud, filling the air with noise and excitement as they rang out their music of high notes and counterpoint of low bass notes.

Amid the ringing of the bells we went on to find the hotel which happened to be a little beyond and across the street from the church and monastery. We got a room easily since we were the only guests. The room was exceptionally large, located on the first floor in what we would call a daylight basement at home. However, here it was more basement than daylight, somewhat like a dungeon. I asked our hotel manager about the *fiesta*, but she just shrugged her shoulders and uttered the usual barrage of Spanish. When we emerged from our room the bells had stopped ringing, and we decided to visit the church that had, so far, dominated our visit.

The front entry was closed, not used, but a side entry was open and we entered the dark interior about half way down the nave. As our eyes adjusted to the gloom we noticed that a service was in progress near the altar, so we retreated in the opposite direction to await the end of the service. Near us, in an alcove, Virgin Mary and baby Jesus were lit by strings of Christmas tree lights, and a tinny-sounding music box played a menu of Christmas carols, endlessly. One of which was Rudolph the Red Nosed Reindeer.

"I think we have another funeral." whispered Doris. "Can you see the casket near the altar?"

"No," I whispered back, "it's too dark for me to see, but I doubt that it's another funeral. This village is too small to have back-to-back funerals."

"Well, I can see a casket," she whispered.

Our whispers were loud enough to turn the heads of a couple people in the audience nearest us, so after that, we sat quietly waiting for the service to end. We didn't want to attract any more attention to ourselves by walking out. Coming in and whispering was bad enough. We sat long enough to hear the music box run through the carols about three times before the service ended, abruptly.

Out came the boys, then men carrying lighted candles. Women followed carrying green fronds, and sure enough, four men carrying a casket. Doris was right. We were the sole onlookers at the start of a second funeral procession. Again we tried to disappear. This time into the gloom of the church but, unfortunately, we stood out quite clearly in the reflected glory of Christmas tree lights along with Virgin Mary and Baby Jesus. They came up the aisle toward us, turned, and passed in revue out the side door where another band began to serenade them on the long walk to the cemetery.

We were probably the most talked-about subject in the village that night. The bells above us began to peel out Te-dums, and the large bell with its single bass note tolled the mournful message. And in back of us a tinny-sounding "Rudolph" played again. It must have been a very unhappy Christmas for many in this village. Yet, even as the bells attested to death, Rudolph attested to life. Those tinny little Christmas songs continued on and on, long after the majestic bells fell silent.

Perhaps, I thought, *death should be considered as just a passing shadow, whereas life, like a music box, went on, and on, and on.*

We poked around the church and the abandoned monastery for a while, climbing three sets of stairs to the roof for views out over the hot, arid countryside. We didn't stay too long out in the intense heat of the sun and retreated to the shaded corridors of the monastery. We walked down endless corridors past little monkish doors on one side, and an open courtyard on the other, where fast growing shadows formed as the sun settled in the western sky. The arched doors—with height so low even Doris, at five feet, four inches, had to duck to get through them—opened into bare, little rooms. They were empty except for a small crucifix set in its own niche in the harsh stone wall. The courtyard garden was unkempt and in disarray, but still it's greenery was a welcome contrast to the white limestone walls of the monastery and the drab desert beyond the walls.

Late in the afternoon we found the only restaurant in the village, but the door was locked. We knocked anyway and, in a few minutes, found ourselves seated at one of two tables set in the middle of a store. They provided us no menu. We simply ate what the family had for dinner that night: tortillas sprinkled with a few pieces of chicken and cheese under a bit of hot salsa. Along with that, we got the inevitable beans plus a bottle of cold beer, each. We sat alone in the quiet store/restaurant listening to low murmurs of conversation and laughter coming from somewhere in the house beyond the next room. Little children giggled as they peeked at us from behind the door leading into the house.

The dinner was very good and, with beer, cost $1.50 each. It was an amazingly low price. The cook also knew about the *fiesta*, and that seemed even more amazing at that point.

"Oh, *si*," she said in English, mixed with Spanish. "It is *manana* in the *Catredal* from twelve o'clock to one o'clock."

"It's only a church service," I moaned to Doris after we left. "No parade, no fireworks, and certainly no rodeo."

"It might be a lot of fun sitting in the Cathedral, listening to people speaking in Spanish," said Doris with a sideways glance at me and a hint of a crooked smile on her face.

We walked back home through the dark and quiet village and decided that what we had experienced that day was probably far more interesting than a one-hour church service. So, we left early the next morning, and never did see the *fiesta* at Coixtlahuaca.

Sleeping Well in Dracula's Town, Romania

The train was late. Twilight proclaimed the coming darkness when we arrived at the station in Sighisoara, Romania. The town touted its claim to fame as the birthplace of Vlad Tepes, otherwise known as Dracula. I'm always a little anxious arriving in a strange town after dark, especially in a foreign country. I have a hard enough time orienting myself during the daylight, even more after dark. But added to that, I couldn't help thinking of Dracula's minions lurking in the shadows watching our delicious necks go by.

Doris and I picked out a couple hotels from the guidebook to try for a room that night. Normally, we asked directions and walked to a hotel, but with night approaching in Dracula-land we decided to get a taxi and let the driver find the hotels.

The few passengers who got off the train with us quickly disappeared in the gloom, and I felt abandoned. They went home, or at least knew where they were going, but we remained unsure. We went out the front of the station and down some stairs to the street. No taxis were in sight, and no people, except a solitary woman loitering near the bottom step. As we started to pass she spoke to us in Romanian, I think, and made a pantomime of resting her head on her hands as though her hands were a pillow.

"Isn't that sweet," said Doris. "I think this little old lady is offering us a room for the night."

Old? Shoot, I bet she's our age.

I took another look around at the empty street.

So, what could we do? We could wait for a taxi, or walk into town. Or we could go with this sweet little old lady.

Turning to the woman, I asked, "How much?" while holding up one hand and rubbing my thumb lightly across the tip of my middle and index fingers.

She understood and said something in Romanian while holding up one hand. I counted five fingers which to me meant fifty thousand lei, in Romanian currency. At the exchange rate of seven thousand two hundred lei per dollar, that worked out to be about seven dollars for the room. Not taking any chances for misunderstanding I whipped out paper and pen, and gave them to her. Then made scribbling motions on the palm of my hand with my fingers. She understood and laboriously wrote on the paper.

"Old, my foot," I said to Doris in a low voice. "I betcha she's about our age. We're in our late sixties and we're not old."

"Well, she looks older than us," said Doris.

"The price is right," I told Doris, after the woman had finished writing fifty thousand. "But, we can always turn it down if the room doesn't look good."

"Okay, let's go, I guess," said Doris, glancing over her shoulder at the cheerfully lit railroad station.

I said, "Yes," to the Romanian lady and nodded in case "yes" in Romanian was a different word. She smiled at Doris, and before leading us down the street she pointed to herself and said "Valie," then some Romanian pointing to Doris.

Doris pointed to her own chest, and said, "I'm Doris." And then pointing to the Romanian lady, said, "and you're Valie."

Valie's smile widened as she nodded vigorously. Both women hugged, and that seemed to cement the deal. We walked about four blocks to Valie's house set behind a six-foot high solid board fence right at the sidewalk. In the semi-dark it showed up as bright green in the light of the street lamp across the way. She invited us in through a pedestrian door set in a larger vehicular gate across a driveway where we met her husband. He spoke even less English than Valie, which wasn't much, and let her do the talking.

The living area was on the second floor accessed by an outside stairway. We entered a small sitting room filled with large potted plants, almost like entering a greenhouse with the same earthy smell of plants gone crazy. Squeezed among the foliage were a couch, a chair, and a coffee table with just enough space to get through it all. A double door led into a large dining room crammed with big heavy furniture. I noted a table with chairs seating ten, a sideboard, an armoire, a couple of dresser drawers, and a large ornate couch filled with pillows of bright colored needlework. The furniture was made of beautifully carved wood with a finish that showed off its natural grain. I felt like I was in museum. Again, we had barely enough room to walk around. I thought maybe they had once lived in a bigger house, and were now storing the furniture in a smaller place rather than discard such beautiful heirlooms.

Two bedrooms opened off on one side of the dining room, and the bathroom was on the opposite side across from the bedrooms, through the obstacle course of furniture. It appeared to be a later addition. Valie offered us a choice of either bedroom. Whichever one we chose, she and her husband would sleep in the other. I chose the one nearest the exterior door. I suppose I felt safer nearer the outside door in case we needed to bail out in an emergency. Doris said it was a "man thing."

We dropped our stuff in the bedroom, said a quick goodbye to Valie, and went out to find a restaurant while a remnant of daylight still remained. We retraced our route back to the train station, now looking dark and gloomy without the lights on, and turned right toward the town center. I had a small-scale map from our guidebook to help me find the way. Doris doesn't read maps very well, so I tended to lead and she followed.

Part way down the street, before we saw them, we heard the noises of children playing in the street. Their shouts and screams pierced the calm evening.

"Why do little girls have to scream when they play?" I asked.

"I don't know," said Doris. "Maybe they're practicing to deal with you men later on."

I couldn't think of an appropriate response, so I stayed quiet.

When we came in sight, the kids stopped playing to watch us. They looked like third or fourth graders, and stood in a clump near the sidewalk like little jaybirds. Or were they crows? A streetlamp lighted the scene, and the open doorways of houses a few feet off the sidewalk contributed some light. It was a warm evening in Romania.

"Hallo," called out a boy before he jumped back trying to disappear into the group numbering six to eight kids.

"Hello," said Doris.

This brought out a chorus of hellos, and then the inevitable question.

"Where are you from?"

"The United States," Doris replied.

"America," rippled through the group, and that opened up a cascade of questions.

"Do you like our country?"

"Where are you going?"

"Are you staying here?"

"Do you have children back in America?"

"How long will you be in our country?"

The noise and laughter brought a couple of the moms out to the sidewalk curious to see the cause of all the commotion that was so different from the normal sounds of play.

"Do you have a restaurant near here?" I asked one of the moms, making a pantomime of eating.

They shook their heads and then tapped their fingers on their mouth, waving them off and shrugging. No English, I guessed. But their children translated for us, and after the moms consulted among themselves, a solemn-looking girl stepped forward. She was the tallest of the kids, pretty skinny, and perhaps nine or ten years old.

"Keep going down street," she said, waving an arm in that general direction. "Cross the river. After that, come to a park. In there is a restaurant."

Doris talked and laughed with the kids about their school and play, and answered questions about what it was like in the United States. They swarmed close about her, sometimes yelling for her attention. Finally, I got Doris to break it off. She would have stayed talking to the kids all night.

"Goodbye," Doris said as we started to walk away.

Back came a chorus of enthusiastic goodbyes, and a couple of the boys trailed us a short distance to make sure we heard their goodbyes.

"Those kids know English," I said.

"No kidding," said Doris. "They must be learning it in school, because their moms don't speak a word of it."

"That's strange, because I halfway expected to hear Russian, not English."

As instructed, we came to the river, crossed it, and found an open grassy area, the park, a short distance away from the river. Looking around we found a restaurant at one corner of the park. It served mostly pizzas, so we ordered a medium one to share. That's when we learned Romanian portions were a lot less than American. Their medium pizza was about the size of our small pizza back home. I wasn't hungry enough to order a second one, but I figured I'd come to the right country to lose weight. When we left the restaurant, I turned right, but Doris walked off to the left.

"Where are you going?" I asked, walking on.

"I'm going back to our room. Where are you going?"

"You're going the wrong way," I said, as I continued walking slowly, thinking that she'd catch up to me.

"No I'm not. You're going the wrong way."

"I know I'm right," I said. "Besides, I've got the map."

By now we were on opposite sides of the park and had to shout back and forth. *What has gotten into that woman? Normally, I lead, and she follows. This is crazy.*

"Doris!" I yelled as softly and persuasively as I could. "Come walk with me. I miss you. If we're lost, wouldn't it be more fun to be lost together rather than lost separately?"

After a few seconds, she cut across the park to where I was and said, "I'll go along with you until you find out you're wrong."

We came to the bridge and crossed the river, but I didn't say a word. Part way up the street where we had talked to the children, she finally spoke.

"I would have gotten here my way, you know, but yours was faster. I knew it was over here someplace."

I smiled and chuckled to myself. *How can a guy argue with that kind of logic?*

We got back to the familiar green fence, and when we went in, Valie was there to greet us. She followed us upstairs talking to Doris in Romanian and pantomiming. I don't know if Doris had the slightest idea what she was saying, but she smiled and nodded. That seemed to satisfy Valie, because she went on talking.

We had noticed before that weavings and many pieces of needlework covered the walls of the dining room. Now Doris pointed to them and then pointed to Valie who gave her a beaming smile and nodded vigorously. Valie made motions of sewing something in her hand and pointed to Doris, whose turn it was to smile and nod vigorously.

Valie went to one of the many drawers in the room and carefully brought out other pieces of completed needlework and many works in progress. Soon they were sitting side by side on the sofa talking the international language of needlework. They laughed, compared colors of thread, and poured over various stitches as if they were old time friends sharing their knowledge of needlework. I watched for a while and finally went off to bed and read.

The next morning in full daylight, we saw a mass of intertwining grapevines supported overhead on a wire and wood trellis. Their leaves shaded the entire driveway, and myriad bunches of pale green grapes hung down like miniature, translucent chandeliers. Doris made friends with the family's big shaggy dog, and I watched the chickens pecking their way across the yard. Valie also had two cats who purred their way around Doris's ankles, and several rabbits in cages who twitched their noses at us as we walked by. She and her husband were eating in the kitchen which was on the lower floor right under our bedroom. We waved as we went out looking for food. I was starving.

We went past the restaurant of the night before, still closed, so we walked on into the center of town. It consisted of four or five blocks of stores on both sides of the street, but no restaurants that we could see. We peered into all the store windows looking for food. Each store window displayed a hodgepodge of a few items for sale, everything and anything.

We might see a few canned goods stacked in a pyramid next to a pair of shoes, next to some tools, next to some hardware goods. In another store window we might see a little produce, next to a couple of dresses, next to a piece of meat, next to some ballpoint pens. We entered several stores in our quest for food, and found that the goods displayed in the window represented most of their entire stock. The store, otherwise, was embarrassingly empty.

We finally found a place with lots of men standing around a counter drinking coffee dispensed from a large urn. They had rolls for sale to go with the coffee, so that was our breakfast.

The medieval town of Sighisoara with its intact walls, towers, and sixteenth century houses, lay on a hill above the city center. Supposedly, it was the birthplace of Vlad Tepes—known as Dracula, dragon—after his father, Vlad Dracul. The infamous name of Tepes, the Impaler, came from Dracula's habit of impaling his captured enemies. These included a lot of Turks who were the big threat to Romania at the time. So, Dracula was a national hero for a while until his own people became tired of being impaled along with the Turks. About four hundred years later, in the nineteenth century, he became the inspiration for the fictional character of Count Dracula, invented by Bram Stoker.

We found Dracula's house. At least that's what the sign outside said, and we stepped inside to see how he lived. Rough-cut stone formed the thick walls of his house. A narrow passageway led from the entry to an open area dimly lit by a couple small windows set high off the floor that perforated the thick walls. In it were several tables and chairs, and a rudimentary bar.

"It's a tavern," I exclaimed. "Well, why not?"

Doris and I sat and had a beer in what, perhaps, was Dracula's living room. Late in the afternoon we climbed to the top of the ridge across the tracks from Valie's house to eat at a fancy restaurant with a great view of Sighisoara and purported to have the best food in town. We sat outside at a bare wood picnic table, and ate a set dinner, no menu, no choices. While the view was great, the food was not memorable, a little piece of chicken, a few pieces of boiled potato, some cabbage, and a plate of bread. Again, disappointed by the meager portions, I loaded up on bread.

"This is a sparse meal," said Doris, looking around for more.

"These Romanians don't seem to eat much," I replied.

When we left the next morning to catch our train, Valie insisted we come back in the fall. She wanted us to help harvest the grapes and make wine. I don't think she really understood how far apart we were. *Not much chance of us getting back here,* I thought, *but you never know.* She and Doris hugged and cried a little, and then we went away.

Vallie rests in front of her kitchen.

Sleeping Better in Dracula's Town: Romania

We arrived in Sighisoara on the same train as we had seven years before. This time it wasn't late, and bright daylight kept the shadows at bay. *No minions of Dracula could exist here,* I imagined. Many passengers got off who were mostly tourists, like us. A lot of them were young adults, easily distinguished by their super large packs compared to the small light packs Doris and I carried. In our mid-seventies, I didn't think both of us, working together, could lift, much less carry, one of those monstrous packs. Age had a way of limiting how many clean shirts and underwear we were willing to carry.

Knots of young people stood around on the platform looking at guidebooks and discussing the next steps to take. Doris and I had already picked out a couple hotels from our guidebook to try for a room, and since we had been here before, we knew the way. Besides, we might run into Valie again and stay at her house as we did seven years before. As we walked away from the train along the platform, two boys spoke to us in good English. I thought they were about fourteen years old.

"Do you need a room?" one asked.

"We know a nice place," the other chimed in. He was walking a bicycle.

"Yes, it is close" said the first.

I nodded and said, "Yes, we need a room."

We kept walking toward the front of the station while I asked them the cost, just how close was their idea of close, and what kind of place was it? A private room in a house, a hotel, or what?

"It is a hostel," said the first boy who seemed to be in charge. "It is very new, not in your guidebook yet. Come with me, you will see. It is very close."

Doris and I consulted quickly.

"Do you think Valie is still taking travelers into her house?" asked Doris.

"Well, she isn't here soliciting. And, she only had the one bedroom which I doubt would be much competition for a new hostel in the neighborhood."

We decided to go with the two boys. After all, we could always decline the room if it was a dud, and walk to the hotels we had picked, or try to look up Valie. Outside the station the boy with the bike said goodbye and rode off.

"What's your name," asked Doris with her usual big smile.

"I am Alex," he said, pointing to his chest and grinning at Doris.

Alex led us past Valie's house where we had stayed before. She had repainted her fence in a tan color instead of the bright green I remembered. About two blocks beyond we came to a house, now converted to a hostel. It was so new that a man was still in the process of painting its name, "Hostel Elena" on the wall facing the street.

A robust, energetic woman bustled out to greet us loudly in German. Her name was Elena, as in Hostel Elena. She seemed a little disappointed to find that we spoke only English. However, Elena recovered quickly, and enthusiastically showed us a room, all the while gesturing and talking in a boisterous combination of broken English mixed with German and, I think, some Romanian thrown in. We agreed to take the room, and she insisted we follow her out of the hostel, right now, immediately. We had just time enough to drop our packs in the room before she practically pushed us out and led us into her backyard.

The backyard was a complete outdoor tavern, enclosed by a six-foot high solid board fence with a gate at the rear for friends and neighbors to slip in and out. Pictures and travel posters in bright colors and patterns covered the fence, and helped make the yard look festive. A few customers sat at picnic tables with drinks in hand, chatting. Alex, our guide was there and greeted us in English. In one corner a small bar displayed its available labels protected in its own separate cave-like shelter. It looked similar to those small roadside alcoves set up for offerings and prayers. I halfway expected to see a cross and a picture of Jesus prominently displayed in front of the bottles. On the opposite side of the yard a large brick barbecue sat under a wood roof. Two huge umbrella-like awnings covered the picnic tables and much of the yard, so that in a rain no one would get too wet walking from the bar to the tables to the barbecue. There, we met Elena's husband, Dorian, who greeted us in a friendly, jovial manner.

"I run the bar." he said. "Anything you want out here, just ask me. Elena takes care of everything inside, and that's how we share the work."

"Share the work, my foot," said Doris to me later in a low voice. "Dorian's got the best part of the deal. Any man would rather guzzle a little beer with his cronies than make a bed or clean a toilet."

Alex and a couple of the customers at one table made room for us to sit, and we each ordered a beer. But before we could drink it, Elena came over with a bottle of *slivovitz*, the powerful plum brandy favored by the Romanians. She filled shot glasses for us and one for herself with the fiery liquor. Then she gave us a welcoming toast, heartily echoed by everyone there. We sat and talked with help from Alex who translated English and Romanian. The first round of *slivovitz* was so good, Elena poured a second shot for us, before excusing herself to go inside, and fulfill her share of the workload of running the hostel.

Dorian carried on outside by lighting festive Japanese lanterns and some colored lights that highlighted the bar making it look even more like a cave. With that labor finished, he got himself a beer and sat with us until interrupted by the orders for drinks as several more ladies and a few men slipped in through the back gate. They filled the tables, stood at the bar, and sat on plastic patio chairs. All seemed to know each other, and they filled the backyard with talk and laughter. As the only strangers there, and Americans at that, Dorian introduced us to everyone who came which kept Alex busy translating.

Finally, I told Doris, "I'm hungry. Let's go out and get something to eat"

"Well, it's past eight," Doris said, "and I sure need a break from this partying."

"No, no, stay here and eat," said Dorian. "I'll get Elena to bring you out something."

But Elena didn't have anything to bring out, and I think she was a little embarrassed.

"If you eat here tomorrow," she said, "I can go to the market in the morning, and then cook dinner for you."

Doris and I agreed. Elena and I negotiated the price for dinner the next evening. Doris let me handle the money, because she hardly ever knew what the foreign currency was worth. A lousy bargainer, she let me do all the haggling.

"Now you must hurry to the store," said Dorian. "It closes very soon. You must get some meat, and I will cook it for you on the barbecue."

We protested, not wanting to impose on his hospitality.

He laughed and shook his head.

"You go, and I start a fire."

"It's no bother for him," said Elena, waving her arm in an off-hand manner. "I'll fix a salad to go with your dinner."

Again, we negotiated price, this time for two salads.

"Now you must go," said Dorian, fussing with some

wood and kindling at the large brick barbeque. "Alex will show you the way."

Alex led us through the back gate, across some empty lots to a side street. It ended in about two blocks in front of a small food store, somewhat like a convenience store and deli combined. They had no fresh meat, but we located several dubious looking pieces of meat in a frozen food case. We picked out something that looked familiar, frozen hamburger.

"That is *mititie*," said Alex who seemed pleased with our choice. "Very good."

When we got back to the yard party, many of the guests had gone, so Dorian had plenty of time to cook our meat.

"Very good meat," he said, echoing Alex's approval.

What was so very good about frozen hamburger? I thought. By this time Doris and I were curious to know why Romanians said it was so great. Elena brought us our salads, made of cut-up tomatoes, cucumbers, onions, and olives. The smell of the meat cooking on the grill was to die for. Someone told me years before that the wonderful smell of cooking meat was simply burning fat. I usually discounted that unpleasant fact. Then Dorian served the first of the savory grilled meat which he had shaped into one inch diameter rolls, about three inches long.

"Oh my, this is delicious," said Doris.

"Wow," I said, "this isn't like any hamburger I've ever had. Do you think it's just beef or mixed with some other kind meat?"

The smell alone was wonderful, and neither of us

could figure out what was in the meat to make it taste so good. We easily ate it all. Later, Elena wrote down the recipe to take home with us:

- 2# ground beef, ground-up
- 3/4# Suet
- Garlic
- Baking soda
- Juniper berries
- Caraway
- Meat broth
- Salt and pepper

"Suet? I hate to think it's the suet that makes this taste so good," I said. "Good grief, I didn't know anyone cooked with that stuff anymore."

"I have some old recipes at home that use suet," said Doris.

"Well, maybe someday I'll try the recipe without the suet and see if it tastes as good as I remember."

I never did, and since I do all the cooking for dinners at home, it's my fault.

Partway through dinner, Alex said goodbye to us. He wanted to go home to watch the soccer game between Greece and Croatia. Shortly after that, Dorian broke out his guitar and played some foot-stomping folk tunes. More customers had drifted in through the back gate, and soon people were singing, and lifting glasses in toasts.

"*Bafta*," cried out a man sitting at our table.

Several others responded with "*Bafta,*" but I called out "Cheers."

"No, no, no," said the man. "It's *Bafta, Bafta,*" and he raised his glass in my direction.

What the heck, I thought, and I raised my glass. "*Bafta.*"

Back came applause and approval from the others with lots more *baftas.*

"He is a Gypsy man," said Dorian. "They say that when making a toast. We Romanians say 'Noroc,' but both mean the same thing."

The Gypsy man got up and danced with one of the women. Dancing to the folk music, their gyrations were a little more sedate and stylized than rock and roll, but only just a little. Before long, he had Doris up there dancing with them which was not hard to do, since she loved to dance. Many times when music started she just naturally began bouncing around. It was easy to get her going, and in the past, I've come home to surprise her pirouetting about the living room to music loud enough to drown a boom box.

When the other lady quit, the gypsy-man and Doris danced on to the approval of all. I figured Dorian owed her a beer on the house for providing so much entertainment for his customers. At seventy-six, I couldn't figure how she could keep on throwing her body around, but she did, until Dorian temporarily quit playing to quench his thirst. *Pretty thirsty work playing that guitar.* Then the Gypsy man gave Doris a hug and peck on the cheek. He quickly looked over at me to see if his actions had offended me, but I raised my glass and called out, "*Bafta.*" The Gypsy man danced on alone, and couldn't entice Doris with a repeat performance. *Maybe at last, she was tired.* We laughed and talked to the others a little while longer, but I was fading fast. When we finally went to bed, Doris didn't object.

I was a little slow getting up the next morning. Fortunately, I didn't have to engage my mind to negotiate a price for breakfast. The cost of the room included that.

"How are you feeling?" asked Doris, bright-eyed and grinning. "One too many *baftas* last night?"

I didn't respond. A little later, Elena took us to a large open-air market filled with temporary stalls overflowing with produce, fruit, and meat. With her help we bargained for fruit and cheese for our onward journey the next day, and then left Elena shopping while we went exploring in the town of Sighisoara.

We walked through the center of town, and found it filled with people including a lot of tourists. The town had changed from our visit here seven years before. We came across several crowded restaurants with extensive menus. The stores were full of items and their windows indicated their specialties. Dress shops, or groceries, or hardware, or drugs. They no longer sold a hodgepodge of a few scarce items that we remembered from before.

"Nothing stays the same," I sighed.

"I think you were complaining before about not finding food, and stores that had little to sell," said Doris.

"Well, the town was kind of quaint," I said. "Now

it's bursting with people and goods. Capitalism gone rampant."

"I never heard of people wanting to stay quaint," said Doris. "They want what we have at home."

"You mean, traffic, noise, and pollution? Rudeness and commercialism? Telemarketing and people walking around with a phone stuck to their ear?"

"I was thinking of a plentiful supply of food," said Doris, "and nice clothing, and places where we women can get beautiful for you grumpy old men."

When we walked up to the old town perched on the hill above the more modern city, I found plenty of quaintness. Tourists were there too, but they congregated on the main streets and by walking away in any direction a few blocks, we left them behind. In a short distance we invariably ran into the original defensive walls and watchtowers that surrounded the old town. Dating from the fourteen hundreds they looked intact, ready to repel the Turks again should they dare to invade. Completely alone, we walked beside the old walls past houses with yards backing to the wall. We poked around some of the old towers, and enjoyed neat views of the countryside.

In late afternoon we had tea with Lori, a Hungarian woman we met at the hostel's backyard party the night before. Lori spoke good English, and she and Doris got to know one another pretty well. Well enough for Lori to invite us to her house. A little stout woman in her late fifties, Lori moved to England for a while, and was now living close to a daughter in Sighisoara.

"Are you enjoying your stay here?" Lori asked.

"Yes," said Doris.

"It's sure changed a lot since we were here before," I said. "Lots more tourists and shops than when we were here seven years ago"

"Well, come back again in another seven years and you'll see even more changes. The government is planning to build a world-class amusement park, like Disneyland, using Dracula as its theme. You'll see even more tourists then."

"That'll be the death knell of quaintness around here," I said for Doris's benefit.

The apartment was on the third floor, and consisted of a dining room with a small kitchen attached, a living room, and a bedroom. An enclosed porch extended across the front of the apartment to form a narrow room. All the windows were open and a slight breeze circulated around the room, making it the best place to be sitting around on that hot day.

I declined tea, not my favorite drink, but accepted a cold beer. Doris made sure I was happy and comfortable in this pleasant little room, and Lori tuned the TV into a daytime Romanian soap-box drama. Then she and Doris went off into the dining room to have tea and talk. I heard their laughter occasionally above the noise of the TV.

That night we ate the dinner Elena had prepared for us: roast chicken, mashed potatoes, and cabbage salad. But before we ate, she poured us each a glass of slivovitz, thereby ensuring the meal would be great. Afterward, we joined the eternal party in the backyard hosted by Dorian doing his job as life of the party. We stayed awhile, but I was partied-out, so we left early to go to bed. Going past Elena's kitchen she suggested settling our bill, and after some negotiation of the charges, I paid-up in full. Then, before we could leave the kitchen, she insisted we try some food she was cooking for Sunday's dinner the next day. I was already aware of the mouth-watering smells coming from the stove, but I declined. My head was too weary for additional negotiation of charges for this added treat.

"Please, you must try a little of this," she said, "Since you won't be here for Sunday dinner."

I finally figured this offer was a freebie, so we sat at her big table in her warm kitchen while she served us the best of her cooking made for a special day, Sunday. First we ate a bowl of red cabbage soup, slightly sour, but sweet, too, and absolutely delicious. Then came a couple cabbage rolls stuffed with *mititie,* and I groaned with pleasure and the agony of being too stuffed myself.

The next morning Elena shuffled out of her bedroom in her bathrobe and slippers to feed us breakfast. I think she may have partied a little late the night before in her backyard. While feeding us she touted the virtues of Hostel Elena and asked us to send other travelers her way. *Business as usual.* Then she mumbled a goodbye and went back to bed. When finished eating, we gathered up our stuff and let ourselves out, quietly shutting the door behind.

On the way to the train station we passed Valie's house behind its solid board fence where we had stayed seven years before. I couldn't help comparing her tearful goodbye then to Elena's off-handed goodbye this morning.

"We can't leave Sighisoara without seeing Valie," said

Doris, stopping in front of her gate. "She'd never forgive us."

"If she doesn't know we're here, what's there to forgive?" I asked. Then I went on with my usual logic: "She's probably not up yet. She won't remember us. We can't really visit because we don't want to miss our train."

But it didn't matter; Doris was already knocking on the gate. It opened almost immediately, and there was Valie looking the same as we remembered. She gave Doris a welcoming hug, and insisted they sit together a few minutes near the gate to talk. Of course, neither understood the others' language. They hadn't learned a word of each other's language in seven years, but it didn't matter. I stood fidgeting in the drive under the same canopy of grapevines loaded with grapes hanging down, and watched the chickens pecking about. A shaggy old dog came up to investigate, but I doubt he remembered us. I finally broke into their conversation mentioning the train coming pretty quick. The women said a tearful goodbye, and on the way out Valie again invited us to come back in the fall, harvest the grapes, and make wine.

On the way to catch the train, I asked rhetorically, "Will Valie's little oasis withstand the coming changes from Dracula's park?"

"I'm sure it will," said Doris. "Some things never change."

Dorian, the life of the party, and Doris dancing with a gypsy man.

Jeep across the Andes:
Bolivia to Chile

The trip was over before it started. Our jeep stopped where the road disappeared into the water. Ahead of us a huge lake extended for as far as I could see covering a saltpan that according to the guidebook was about forty-six thousand square miles, almost the size of Connecticut. Relatively, a lake that size in the US would cover the state of Virginia.

"Where did all this water come from?" I asked in amazement. "I thought we would be driving over a flat salt desert."

"Well, it sure looks flat," said Doris.

"Come on, all lakes are flat. I'm talking about the water. The road across the saltpan is flooded, and I bet we haven't gone more than twenty miles. You'd think they'd know the road conditions this close to town."

"Maybe we're waiting for a boat," said Doris

The closest town was Uyuni, Bolivia, where we had arrived the night before after a long bus ride from Potosi, the highest city in the world at just over 13,400 feet. The saltpan in front of us was above 12,200 feet, high enough to make my broken heart race trying to pump enough blood around my body. Doris had no such problems; she was healthy as a horse.

We had come to Uyuni, the last major city in Southwest Bolivia because I got this neat idea of taking a shortcut by going overland from the remote southwest area of Bolivia to the Atacama Desert in Northern Chile.

"Let's see if we can get over the Andes to Chile," I said to Doris, making it sound like a piece of cake.

"Okay," she said immediately.

"It may not be so easy to do," I warned, "because we have to go through a primitive area with no buses or major roads that I know of.

"If there's no bus, are we going to hitchhike?" she asked.

"I don't think there are any cars going that way, either."

"Then how can we get through?"

"Tour companies run excursions into that rough area for tourists to visit various wondrous sights. We'll tell them we want to go through the Andes to San Pedro, Chile, just a little way across the border."

Doris looked kind of doubtful, but she rarely questioned my ideas concerning itinerary. Usually, she didn't know where she was anyway. In this case, I didn't think she had a clue where Chile was located in relation to Bolivia, and I tried to explain.

"Chile is the next country directly west of us," I said pointing in the direction of the setting sun.

"Oh, I thought that's where it was," she said. "I knew it was around here someplace."

Uyuni was a small town, and first thing in the morning we easily found a place that signed us up on a jeep tour along with five other people. It would drop us off at the border where we could meet up with another vehicle to take us on into Chile. The entire trip would take three days.

"But what if another vehicle doesn't show-up?" asked Doris.

"Oh something will come along. If not, we'll just go back the way we came."

"How can we do that if we're dropped off, and the jeep's gone back to its home? It's not going to wait to see if we get picked up, is it?" Doris asked nervously.

"Hey, Doris, it's a road, and something's bound to come along sometime. Besides, the people that signed us up said we shouldn't have to wait too long."

She didn't hear my last comments, because she had already started talking to the other women that were going on the trip. They were discussing more exciting and important things than worrying about getting a ride in the middle of nowhere, three days from now.

By mid-morning we had picked up food and water, a gas-fired stove, sleeping bags, and the cook. Before leaving town we helped the driver fill six five-gallon cans with gasoline. We stowed all that stuff including our packs, onto the roof of the jeep and covered everything with a tarp.

"Looks like there are not too many gas stations along the way," said Doris.

"Probably not too many on the way back either," I had replied.

But right now, stuck on the shore of a lake, I expected the driver to turn around and head back to town. We'd get a refund, of course, and then begin a long detour north before we could head west again toward Chile. Three other jeeps joined ours parked where the waters began. The passengers milled about wondering what would come next. The drivers peered under the hoods, fussed with their jeeps, and placed leafy fronds in front of the radiators.

"Why are you doing that?" I asked.

The answer came back in Spanish, and I guess it had something to do with protecting their radiators which didn't make any sense. I dealt with a lot of responses I couldn't quite understand, because I spoke so little Spanish. Just then a public bus came rattling down the road. It was coated in mud and dust, and stuffed with people. Instead of stopping it plowed on through the water leaving behind a wake to mark its trail.

"My God," I said to Doris, not believing my eyes. "Did you see that bus? I think they're going to take us across the lake in this jeep. Incredible."

"I hope it doesn't get too deep," she said. "What'll we do if the water comes in through the door?"

The bus had almost disappeared, now just a dark speck floating above the water, when the driver called us to get back in the jeep.

Soon after, a flotilla of four jeeps, including ours, embarked on the lake together, each choosing a separate path so they didn't follow in each other's wake. The wheels threw up a bow wave higher than the jeep and we peered out the windows through a solid spray of water. Never in my life had I experienced this way of traveling. I noticed that we bumped along at twenty to twenty-five mph through six to eight inches of water.

"Does the water get any deeper?" I asked.

"Maybe a little more," said the driver. "Thirty to forty centimeters."

Rats, I thought. *What's that in inches?* It took me a minute or two to figure out the depth could be twelve to fifteen inches.

Meanwhile the driver went on to say, "Of course, salt miners excavate holes up to two meters deep to get the salt. We never know where they dig and we can't see below the surface of the water."

I had no trouble converting that to be over six feet of water, more than enough to completely submerge our jeep. Uneasily, I sat watching the waters divide on either side of the jeep waiting for us drop into a mine hole. We drove for miles, and as time passed I got tired of worrying about holes, figuring the driver was probably kidding us anyway. The other jeeps going at their own speeds and directions slowly pulled away. Although they still remained in sight, nothing else of interest was left to see except water and a distant shore. The novelty of driving on water faded.

We sat three across scrunched together in three rows. The backseat had been added to cram in more people, and that row was elevated to clear the rear wheels making it hard to look out the windows. The middle row was the normal rear seat of the jeep. And, in front, the driver and one passenger were squeezed by the hefty cook sitting in the jump seat between them.

"Packed in like sardines," I said.

"Just like those buses in Guatemala," said Doris. "Remember, we sat crammed together six across. I sat with one cheek in the seat and the other wedged in the center of the aisle with a stranger across the way. Shoulder to shoulder, and hip to hip"

"You always say you like to be close to the people."

"Yeah, but not that close."

Our companions were a German couple, two young Swiss women traveling together, and a Danish man. The Germans spoke German, French, Spanish, and English. The Swiss women spoke French, and an incomprehensible Swiss dialect, some German, and a smattering of English. The man from Denmark spoke Danish, French, German, Spanish, and English. Doris and I spoke American which was close enough to English.

After trying to converse in the different languages, and translating for those who didn't understand, English was chosen by consensus as the most universal to use. The driver and the cook spoke only Spanish, and the others would occasionally lapse into using their mother tongue, so translations continued to be necessary.

About noon a pure white island came into sight appearing to float just above the water like a mirage. When closer, we saw that it was a salt island lying a foot or so out of the water with a building on it. The jeep stopped beside the low bank and we all disembarked to stretch our legs and look around while the cook set out lunch. The building was a hotel made of salt blocks with a thatched roof. The lobby furniture, beds, tables and even chandeliers were carved from solid blocks of salt. We ate lunch outside at a picnic table carved from salt, and sat on cold hard benches made of salt, like grainy white rock.

"How come they don't melt in the rain?" asked Doris

"They probably do, eventually. Then they make new ones. Or maybe these are really rock, and just look like salt."

"Well they taste like salt."

"You licked this dirty table?" I asked, aghast.

"No, the bench."

After lunch my heart dropped when the jeep wouldn't start. *Great*. I looked around at the sea of water and the land barely visible in the distance. Leaving us on the island, the driver, with help from the hotel staff splashed through the water a few yards to push-start the jeep. Back on board we joked about what would happen if we got stuck out in the middle of this ocean somewhere. *Gallows humor*.

"This is usually dry," said the driver, waving an arm to encompass the water in front of the jeep. "It rained somewhere last week, and we never know when it might get flooded."

"Do you have a compass on board to navigate through to the other side?" I asked.

"No," he said. "Compasses don't work out here."

"Whoa. How do you know where you're going?"

He didn't explain. Just smiled and shrugged. *Great*, I thought. This was good for more gallows humor about being lost in the middle of a giant lake. On and on we went across the water passing an occasional salt islet off one side or the other of our bow. The other jeeps that had started out with us earlier had disappeared, and we traveled alone on an immense inland sea. I saw no major landmarks to measure our progress, where we had gone, or where we were going. By mid-afternoon I lost sight of land, except for distant mountains that formed the Andes. I was restless and tired of being trapped so close together. I felt uneasy as we crawled along through endless waters knowing this little jeep was my only way out. I forced myself to relax, and talked to the others to help pass the time.

"I've got to go to the bathroom," whispered Doris.

The others had good ears and soon we were talking about how we could relieve ourselves in a cramped jeep with water all around. We men figured we had it better than the women if it came right down to it. More gallows humor. What else could we do except laugh, derive a little fun, and hold it in.

A short time later we drove out of the lake on to a small rocky island. Hot, dry land at last. With a bathroom. A family ran a refreshment stand open on one side, like a lean-to. They sold hot and cold drinks and Bolivian junk food, had a few rooms to rent, and lived full time on the island. Their house as well as all the other structures was made from uncut rocks gathered on the island and set in place without mortar. The colors of the rocks were shades of brown, red, and white resulting in structures pleasing to look at, and that blended into the landscape perfectly. The cracks and crevices between the rocks provided welcome ventilation. All very practical, and beautiful too.

The driver had wisely parked the jeep facing downhill, so when we left he coasted to gain enough speed to start the engine just before we hit the water. Off again. We had changed seats to vary the cramping, and I now had the best seat in the house, the front one, next to the driver. Now, I had a clear view of water and distant mountains without seeing them through spraying water. The downside was the cook's bottom which intruded into my space as well as the driver's.

By late afternoon more gallows humor broke out when someone suggested we might be out on the open sea after dark. A little later all joking stopped when the driver turned on his headlights and, in the gathering twilight, we drove on through water. By now I had lost all sense of the fun and novelty of traveling on water that I had that morning, and was heartily sick of the stuff. I was tired of the cramped jeep too, and the only thing making it all bearable was the camaraderie of the group. We had become good friends in less than a day.

Finally, we made landfall just before complete darkness. We drove up on a tiny spit of land stretching across the water in front of us. It was barely wider than the jeep, and I don't know how far out into the lake it extended. We turned right, and went about a mile before reaching the true shore and a primitive dirt road. Like a net spread across the water the spit snagged and funneled the jeep to dry land. *A primitive navigational aid?* I wondered if it had been man-made. The driver stopped while we piled out to stretch our legs and find our own toilet rooms among the brush.

"Are we in Chile?" asked Doris.

"Not even close," I said. "We won't hit the border until the day after tomorrow."

"Where are we going to stay tonight?" she asked, suddenly taking a more practical interest in the journey.

"I'm sure the driver has a place in mind for us up ahead."

Again we changed seats, and I crammed myself into the elevated rear seat. I found that I could see out the window if I scrunched down in the seat. But there was nothing to see. We drove for hours painfully making our way over the bumpy dirt road through a dark and empty land. Just before ten we reached the tiny village of San Juan de Rosario. I couldn't see much, but a few lights here and there proclaimed we were in a village. Civilization at last.

It seemed to me that other jeeps had arrived before us and had taken the places the driver had in mind for us. He tried four places before finding one that took us in. It included the owner's house and animal sheds, our building, and a toilet house, all in a compound behind a six-foot high, solid board fence.

Our building consisted of four rooms, two on each side of a hallway that had an exterior door at each end. On one side was our room with seven single beds, one for each of us passengers, and a second, smaller room for the driver and cook. Across the way the cook set up her kitchen on the floor in a stark bare room devoid of any furnishings. Next to it was a room with a couple tables and benches, obviously the sitting room and dining room.

Unloading the top of the jeep was a messy job. The protective tarp was caked in mud and dust. But worse, the tarp seemed to trap more dust under it than it shed with the result that everything stored on the roof of the jeep was covered in dirt. Fine dust penetrated our packs coating, among other things, shirts and underwear with dirt. The tarp handled water much better, and the packs were essentially dry except for a few damp spots.

"Everything's wet," wailed Doris, greatly overstating the facts, and completely ignoring the dust among the clothes. She apparently tolerated dirt marginally better than wet.

"It's okay, I said, "stuff dries. Just wait it out."

Seven beds in the one room was a tight fit. The aisles between were barely wide enough for access to each bed. Doris and I grabbed the ones closest to the door by spreading out our sleeping bags. Hopefully, we wouldn't disturb the others getting up to go to the bathroom in the middle of the night. The Swiss women were appalled at the primitive conditions, sleeping so close together in one room. By the time all the people and packs were in, the room was crammed. Doris and I didn't mind, because all we were using the room for was to sleep. And once asleep, it didn't matter how many people were around.

Since supper was at least an hour away, the German man suggested looking around the village for a beer. The

Swiss women declined and lay on their beds resting. So, five of us went looking. Passing the so-called kitchen, I saw the cook kneeling with all her kitchen gear, utensils, and food lying about on the bare floor. She was fussing with some chicken while a pot boiled on the one-burner stove. I didn't hang around to see any more, nor did I want to.

The night was frigid at that altitude, about 10,800, feet and I wore all the extra clothes I had with me. We found a place with lights and noise. Passing by the window we saw travelers, like us, drinking what looked like beer. Before we could get to the door, a Bolivian lady stopped us. She was short and round, wearing the typical red-patterned apron tied around her stout waist. Her hair was jet black, styled in a single braid extending down to her waist. And perched on her head, at least one or two sizes too small, was the typical brown bowler hat worn by most women in Bolivia.

"They no have beer here," she said.

"But, they're drinking something," one of us said.

"No beer," she said. "I have beer. You come to my nightclub. You see."

Nightclub? Quickly consulting among us, we agreed it might be fun to go with her to see a nightclub in this tiny village. She gave us the directions.

"You wait there," she said. "I get keys from daughter's house."

We found her nightclub and saw its name above the door in big bold letters, "Night Little." She came bustling up a minute later and opened up for us.

"My nightclub only for tourists," she said, switching on a single bulb in the ceiling. "No village people allowed here."

"That's pretty exclusive," I said, wondering how many tourists ever got to "Night Little" without the help of our hostess.

The building consisted of one room with a bar across one side leaving space enough for a couple tables and benches. She lit two candles and set them on our table. She set another on the bar before turning off the overhead light. *Beer by candlelight. How neat. How romantic.* Then she went behind the bar, turned on some disco music, and waited for us to order some beer. We each had a beer, and sat talking and laughing. The beer was at room temperature, plenty cold enough. We got another round, but before we could finish it, a boy came to tell us that supper was ready. By the time we got back it had been ready for quite a while. I toyed with cold boiled potatoes, and took a few bites of lukewarm fried chicken that had been sitting on the floor when I saw it last. We didn't sit around long, because of the cold. Doris and I went off to bed to get warm and, incidentally, to sleep. By now, we were into the next day, and I was exhausted.

By mid-morning the following day we were back in the jeep, winding our way through the mountains on a narrow dirt road. Our route led south, paralleling the Chilean border. The further we went the higher we got, and soon we were crossing ridges fifteen thousand feet high or higher. By four thirty we arrived at a hostel sitting alone near Laguna Colorado, and stayed the night there. As the name implied, the waters of the nearby lake were a stunning rusty red color.

The hostel rented several rooms in a row with a covered porch across the front that connected them together. I sat on the porch looking at the view of the red lake and feeling rotten. The driver felt sorry for me and fixed me a *matte de te,* a tea made from chopped up coca leaves, the same stuff used to make cocaine. Such a tea was supposed to help relieve symptoms of altitude sickness, which I didn't think I had. I tried it anyway, but I didn't think tea helped a weak heart which I did have. Altitudes above twelve thousand feet were particularly hard for me. Any walking or movement caused me to breathe heavily, and caused my heart to race. Therefore, I stayed as quiet as I could. The frigid air soon drove me off the porch into our unheated room which seemed a little warmer than the air outside.

This time our room contained four double bunk beds, and Doris promptly appropriated the top bunk of the bed nearest the door. By now, we thought it quite normal to be housed so close together, like one big happy family. We sat around a table just inside the door, where we spent the evening talking, playing parlor games, and eating dinner. We had so much fun and laughter that we didn't feel the need to visit any of the other groups who were staying the night, crammed like us, in the adjacent rooms. One jeep-load per room. We spoke to the other travelers, only in chance meetings, when passing to and from the bathroom.

The last day of the jeep trip was cold and clear like

the others, and I dreaded the long hours ahead cooped up in the jeep again. Long before arriving at some hot springs, I saw the telltale billowing of white clouds of steam wafted high and contrasted vividly against the unblemished, deep blue sky. Far above, they eventually dissipated into fragments to reveal the hidden sky-blue color until the next white puff covered that part of the sky again. When closer, the pungent sulfur fumes made me wrinkle my nose at the disgusting odor of rotten eggs.

Along with their peers from the other jeeps traveling on excursion, our young people changed into bathing suits to lie side by side in hot water just deep enough to cover their bodies. They looked like white sardines lined up in a row, only a little less packed than those in a can. Doris and I sat in the shade of the jeep laying bets on how long it would take for all those white skins to turn red in the fierce sun at our altitude. I had opted out of a hot bath because, by this time, my heart wouldn't let me do much more than just sit.

"Why don't you go in?" I asked Doris.

"I don't have a bathing suit."

"That never stopped you before," I said. "I've seen you a couple times go in the water passing off your underwear as a bikini."

"Well, I don't want to leave you."

Good grief, Doris was too concerned about my health to leave my side for even a few minutes.

"I'm okay," I said, "as long as I don't try to leap tall buildings."

"You're not supposed to be here at these altitudes," she went on. "Dr. Hynes said it was bad for your heart."

"Well, this country fools me. Look around. These rolling hills don't look that high, do they? See the mountains sticking up over there? Now that's high."

"So then, what's the altitude here?" asked Doris.

"My body says it's pretty high."

"How high?" she persisted.

The guidebook says 4,800 meters."

"Well, that doesn't sound so bad."

"See there? That doesn't sound bad to me either. I tend to forget that I've got to multiply meters by three point three to get feet."

"So, how many feet?" she went on, pinning me down further.

"Over 15,800 feet."

She gasped and was silent a few seconds, and then she said slowly, "That's higher than Mount Rainier back home."

"I know. It's higher than any peak in the continental United States."

"What are we going to do?"

'There's nothing we can do, except wait it out. By tonight we should be back in thick air again."

We stopped for lunch at Laguna Verde, an intense blue green lake. The elevation was now 16,500 feet and I couldn't move. I sat in the front seat almost comatose while Doris brought me some food, which I couldn't eat. She hovered about like a mother hen, while I longed for lower elevations.

We said goodbye to the two Swiss women who left our group at that point to join those people in the other jeeps returning to Uyuni. They went back by a different route to avoid the flooded saltpan. Ours was the only jeep to go on toward Chile over a more primitive road at higher and higher elevations.

In early afternoon we arrived at the Chilean border, one of the highest, most Godforsaken border crossings I'd ever seen. The police and custom officials stationed at that place must have felt punished, or banished, like the Russians sent to Siberia. If any greenery existed, it was in a pot in one of their shacks. Otherwise, boulders and scree surrounded their station, and a stiff, persistent wind kept trying to blow it all away.

Our driver gave us a cheery goodbye as he turned his jeep around to go back to Uyuni where we had started three days before. We waited, out of the wind, in the lee of a rock wall for a vehicle to come pick us up, and take us to San Pedro, well inside Chile. Waiting was an act of faith in this part of the world, and our vehicle might show up in a few minutes, a few hours, or not at all.

In about an hour a minivan rattled to a stop near us, and the driver assured us that he would take us to San Pedro. He brought supplies and two fresh border guards with him. Their replacements went with us. He didn't collect any money from us, but I couldn't tell if he was part of the tour, or a government shuttle to service the border. And perhaps, as a courtesy, they picked up stray travelers passing through.

The minivan was spacious compared to the jeep,

and we practically rattled around inside. We went down thousands of feet of elevation. The road became smoother, the air became thicker, and I felt better. Now we speeded through the driest desert in the world with yearly rainfall barely measurable, if at all. Nothing grew anywhere. Nothing to see, just piles of grey gravel and rock. But if I had a choice of where to travel, I'd choose the low dry land desert rather than the high desert of a flooded saltpan.

In mid-afternoon we arrived in San Pedro and said goodbye to our good friends of just three days, going our separate ways and promising to meet again before we left town. We walked to several places looking for a room. The town was jammed with young people with their gigantic backpacks. Rooms were scarce and the prices, accordingly, were way too high. The restaurants were crowded, and the townspeople seemed unfriendly, probably overwhelmed by the influx of so many people. After three days of lonely travel, we were also overwhelmed by all the people.

"Let's get out of here," I said.

"Okay," said Doris, "I'm ready to move on."

We got the last tickets on the last bus out of San Pedro that day, and were sitting in a park waiting to leave, when our Danish friend walked by. He stopped to talk and was surprised that we were leaving so soon. He promised to see us once more before we left, and if possible, tell the German couple that we were leaving.

The hour finally arrived when we had to go catch our bus. Our travel friends hadn't shown-up, and we went to the bus station alone, disappointed. Just as the bus came and as we were waiting in line to board, our companions from the jeep trip, good friends for three days, arrived at the last minute to see us off. Like longtime close friends anywhere the good wishes and farewells were heartfelt. Doris cried a little and I almost wished we could stay and party with them one more time.

But I knew that travel friends were fleeting, just chance encounters as we passed by on our separate ways. We would never see them again or recall their names, but I remember them now, many years later, as if it were just yesterday.

Picnic on a salt island at a table of salt set in front of a hotel of salt.

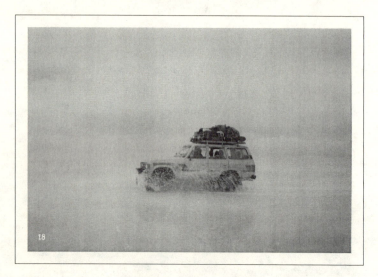

Driving on a salt lake.

Bloody Hell, Americans: South Africa

The second we finished parking on the main street in downtown Beaufort West, South Africa, Doris and I were accosted by two children. A boy and a girl, about fourteen years old, maybe less, carried buckets of water and some rags in their hands. They sloshed soapy water on the windshield and set about washing all the glass on the car.

"Stop," I said, "the windows don't need cleaning."

But it was too late. Most of the glass was covered with soapy water already. To leave them that way would be worse than if they were dirty.

"They're black South Africans," said Doris. "Maybe they don't speak English."

"What's the cost?" I asked, holding up one hand and rubbing my thumb against the first two fingers, the universal sign for money.

"You pay two rands for us each," said the boy pointing at himself and the girl. The girl never looked at us: just kept on working.

"That sounds like pretty good English," said Doris. "How much is that in dollars?"

"Thirty cents apiece."

"We can afford that," said Doris, "Even if our windows were just cleaned."

We had parked as close as possible to the front of a Hostel where we hoped to stay the night. The fortress-like, stone building with the whimsical name of, "Ye Old Thatched Hut," was sandwiched among the wooden storefronts lining the busy street. The town with its one, wide main street felt vaguely familiar, somewhat like our smaller cities in the U.S. Southwest. Dust hung in the air brought in from the surrounding arid plains and low hills. The August day was warm, and I imagined that their summer, occurring here in December and January, could be a scorcher.

We left the teenagers busy washing glass, promising to be back to pay them after getting a room. The entry of the hostel led directly into a dimly lit, rustic-looking dining room with walls of rectangular, rough-cut stone. Primitive handmade tiles decorated the walls in groupings here and there, contrasting their glassy ceramic surface with the crude rock. A huge fireplace, also decorated with a few tiles, dominated one side of the room. In the center of the room, like an island, stood a freestanding wooden structure under a false roof of thatch. A bar opened into the dining room on two of its sides.

It was also the office, the command post for the hostel, and by far the busiest spot in the building. And as the name of the hostel implied, it could be considered a thatched hut, I suppose. A CD by Steve Hofmeyr, South Africa's superstar, blasted away, alternating his hit songs in Afrikaans and English. The warden, or manager, was a young, pretty white woman tending the needs of a few people at the bar who were mostly white.

"What's your pleasure?" she asked in a cheery voice.

"We need a place to stay tonight."

"Well, I have the dorms, of course." Then she grinned and said, "But you would probably be more comfortable in one of my private rooms. You get your car while I open the gate at the side of the building so you can park in the back where your car should be safe for the night."

"Before we came in, two young teenagers started washing our windows before we could stop them," said Doris. "Can you tell us how much we should pay them?"

"Those cheeky little buzzards," said the warden with anger. "Don't pay them one single rand. They're not supposed to be doing stuff like that in town. It's bad for business."

"It's okay with us," said Doris. "Teenagers at home often wash cars to make money."

"Not here," said the warden with a frown. "I'll go out and run them off for you."

"No, no. It's okay. We'll take care of it while you open the gate," I said.

When we got back to the car, the teenagers were nowhere in sight, but they had done their work well. Our glass sparkled, including that on headlights and brake lights. Suddenly, a bus jerked to a stop across the street and our two youngsters dashed over to us, hands out, to collect their pay. Without a word they took our money and streaked back to the bus dodging the heavy, noisy traffic in the street. A second later the bus ground some gears and roared off, disappearing down the street leaving behind its own little cloud of smog.

Later in the evening we sat in the romantic ambiance of a dining room lighted solely by candles set on wall brackets and on the tables. Their soft glow highlighted the imperfections of a wall made of cut stones and mortared joints that created an honest functional beauty. Candlelight merged into shadows, and each table was a separate oasis of light and life. We sat near the huge fireplace now bright with a blazing fire. The only other warm spot in the whole building was the kitchen. I had made a big mistake on this trip thinking South Africa would be warm by mid-August; instead we froze at night and thawed-out during the day. The warden took our orders for supper.

"So, now you're wearing your waitress hat," I commented.

"Yes," she said wearily. "And later you'll see me pushing a mop. It's hard to find anybody to work. You're lucky the cook finally showed up, or you would be trying to eat my lousy cooking tonight. Did you get rid of those little buggers messing with your car?"

"They were gone when we went back outside."

"Good. At least you didn't have to listen to their begging for money."

"But we did pay them," I said. "The bus driver stopped to let them off, and waited until they got back with their pay. That was a nice thing for him to do for just a couple of kids."

"Yes," said Doris, "And, we were glad he did. Work of any kind should be rewarded, don't you think?"

The warden looked surprised. "Bloody hell," she muttered. Then before turning to take orders from the other diners, she shrugged, shook her head, and said, in rueful resignation, "Americans."

Biking Through History: Ireland

From out of the blue, I had a problem—my fault, of course. Doris was really mad. She got off her bike and dumped it to the ground. Then she threw her pack into the middle of the road.

"I'm hungry," she said. "You said we would eat when you found a nice rock to sit on. We've passed hundreds of nice rocks."

That was true, we had. There were so many nice rocks in Ireland it was hard to pick out the best. It was somewhat like picking out the best campsite in a campground full of good campsites. It always took at least one complete drive through. But now I was stuck. I had to get Doris fed and not a single rock in sight except for those way off in the fields. The road we were on was a narrow farm road, paved, with shallow ditches on both sides. Green grass and weeds grew in the ditches and extended beyond them for miles around.

So, we sat on the green grass and weeds with our backs to a fence and our feet in the ditch. No fear of traffic; there wasn't any. We ate our cheese, crackers, and some fruit, and Doris began to mellow a little. She had a sunny disposition most of the time, but you had to keep her fed, or she got mean as a snake. I noticed that trait more often after we passed into our seventies.

We had arrived in Dublin, Ireland a few days before. We walked about savoring some of the pubs, and getting acclimated to life in Ireland. From there we traveled from town to town by bus, with backpacks still considerably smaller than those dragged around by our younger fellow travelers. We found that many of the sights we wanted to see, mostly historical, were located outside the towns and beyond bus stops, many were off in some farmer's field.

That was when we hit upon the idea of using bicycles. Every town had bikes for rent, and we used them to get around the countryside carrying only a light daypack with us. We left our heavier packs with the hotel or hostel where we had stayed the night before, and then picked them up when we returned from our bike ride two to four days later.

With Doris fed, and now back to her normal smiling self again, we got on our bikes and continued our search for a place called Three Castle Head where an old castle was supposed to be located. We came to the end of the farm road which died at the edge of a stony beach. The waves came crashing in all the way from America, and the air smelled of salt spray. The beach was perhaps two hundred feet long and, on each end, large boulders lay jumbled into huge piles. Just beyond those loose rocks, solid sheer cliffs dropped into the ocean. Not a good place to walk about, but a parking lot was located nearby.

"Doris," I said, "this parking area can't be for such a lousy beach, it must be parking for the castle."

"No, we passed it a little way back."

"You mean the castle or parking?"

"The castle."

"I didn't see a sign for a castle."

"I mentioned it to you when we passed, but you never listen to me."

That was a pretty common complaint, and I had learned not to respond to it.

"It was right there," she went on, "a sign on a driveway gate that said *castle.*"

"Wait a minute," I said, "that sign said '*No Trespassing,*' nothing about a castle."

We got on our bikes and went back about half a mile to the driveway and, sure enough, Doris was right. A small sign did say Castle, but the much bigger one told us to stay out.

I was confused. Why advertise a castle and say *keep out?* All we could see beyond the gate was a tidy white farmhouse and outbuildings set back about a quarter mile off the road. Lots of picturesque sheep dotted the slopes above the farm, but no people, and no castle.

"This can't be it," I said. "Where can visitors park their cars and why a 'No Trespassing' sign? And where is the castle?"

"Cool your jets," said Doris, and read the whole sign; it says '*Mizen Castle, temporarily closed due to repairs; no public right-of-way.*'"

"Darn, I didn't see that; it's all in fine print. Now what are we going to do?"

We had started out the day from the youth hostel in Schull. It had been cold and windy with spats of rain the day before and this day didn't look too promising either. We wanted to go to Mizen Head to see the lighthouse on the most southwest point of land in Ireland. We also wanted to see Mizen Castle which was quite close on the next prominent point to the north.

Public buses didn't go to the lighthouse or the castle, so our choices were to hitchhike or rent bikes. We chose bikes which the hostel warden was happy to rent to us. The wind was very strong coming from the west, the direction we needed to go. We weren't too happy about the prospect of pedaling into that wind.

Then, in a stroke of good luck the warden got us a ride to the lighthouse. A special bus had stopped at the hostel the night before and the passengers had stayed the night there. This bus came from England to tour around Ireland on a scheduled route. Passengers could get off at any town scheduled for a stop on the route, stay for any length of time, and get back on when the next bus came through. The passengers had some latitude on what to see along the route and this day they had chosen to see the lighthouse at Mizen Head before going on to the next scheduled stop. Ironically it was their second choice; the first choice of kayaking there at Schull had been canceled because of the strong wind.

We stored our bigger packs with the warden, got our bikes on board the bus, and rode in comfort to Mizen

Head. After visiting the lighthouse, we mounted our bikes and peddled over to Three Castle Head, to end up in a dead end at the no trespassing sign.

"Doris," I said, "let's go in and see the castle anyway."

"No, we can't just go in there. It might be dangerous. They might call the police or have a big, bad dog around. Besides, I don't want to be embarrassed if someone finds us in a place we shouldn't be."

"Well okay," I said, "but I've read about this at home and came eight thousand miles to see this castle. I don't want to just leave without trying. Why don't we at least go up to the house, and if anyone is there, we can ask them about the castle."

"You're the only person I know would go this far to see an old, ruined castle."

"Hey, it's not just the ruins. Sometimes, there's more fun getting there."

"All right, but this makes me very uneasy."

With that I opened the gate and pushed my bike inside before she could change her mind; she had been known to rebel on rare occasions. We both started trudging up the long driveway toward the house. By the halfway point I began to relax a little.

"See Doris, no dogs, no angry shouts, and no police."

"We're not there yet," she said.

"Pessimist," I responded.

Just as we arrived at the path to the front door of the house, the door popped open and a lady came out.

"Good afternoon," she said, "I am so pleased to see

you have come on bicycles. Not many come this way on bicycles."

We explained that we wanted to visit the castle, but we were concerned about the "closed" sign on the gate out at the road.

"Oh, you're Americans. I can tell. You've earned the right to see the castle coming all this way on your bikes."

We didn't tell that we had just started riding our bikes from Mizen Head which was a lot closer than the nearest town, and certainly closer than America.

"Just you go up through that gate and follow the fence line to the upper pasture," she said, waving in the general direction. "Go through another gate and through open country to the ridge, and from there you should see the ruins. I go there quite often; it's only a walk of ten minutes or so."

I looked up at the ridge and figured we would be lucky to make it to the top in thirty minutes, much longer getting to the unseen castle beyond.

"But," the farm lady continued, "I advise you not to go into the ruins, because the standing walls are quite weak and they could fall anytime. You know the castle dates from early in the twelfth century."

We assured her that we would stand well clear of the walls. With that, we parked our bikes against her stone wall and started walking. We were completely alone and on our own, a far cry from our visit to Mizen Head that morning.

At Mizen Head we had joined an army of tourists to walk the trail to the lighthouse at land's end. They came in cars and charter buses and parked in a substantial parking lot. After paying a fee at a gate, we followed the extension of the road, now quite narrow, as it followed the brow of cliffs only to end abruptly at a marvelous suspension bridge.

Walking over this bridge we had views of shaggy, gray, shale cliffs to the north and to the southwest. The cliffs were neatly framed in the void between the mainland and the islet upon which the lighthouse had been built. Other islets were strung along the cliffs, but the lighthouse had been built on the largest. Far below through the open grate of the bridge we saw boiling white waves crash against the cliffs.

The lighthouse was built in the early 1900s. It was no longer active and now existed as a historical site, and for the pleasure of tourists. We joined a guided tour of the facilities which included, an office/sitting room, bedroom, kitchen, and of course, the room housing the revolving light. It was the biggest room and the brightest with all its windows.

By contrast the living quarters were dismally dark and cramped. Our tour group of ten couldn't fit in one room at once, and the small doors and tiny hallways restricted movement from room to room. The interior was furnished as it might have appeared in the early 1900s. Apparently no tower was required for the beacon light which had stopped revolving several years before. From that room we had 270 degrees of unobstructed view from cliffs to the north to cliffs to the southwest. And straight ahead, west, if we could have seen that far, was America.

When we went back over the suspension bridge we stopped again to see the truly awesome sight of vertical cliffs withstanding the onslaught of the waves pounding against their base. Each wave rolled in, one after the other, powerfully, relentlessly, to smash its energy against that immense, immovable rock fortress. Each wave met its end with a roar like a beast in rage, and exploded in frustrated sprays of water sent high in the air in protest, before subsiding in boiling waters in front of the next wave.

The immense cliff stood silent and aloof, disdainful of such petty action at its base. But we knew with certainty that, in time, the waves slowly, but surely, ate away at the base of the cliff until the weight of its own rock became the enemy. Then to ease the tremendous pressure of its weight, a portion of the cliff would crack, and eventually splinter off to make a new islet. I encouraged Doris to take many pictures in a vain attempt to record my feelings of insignificance when measured against such a backdrop of power and timeless age, but back home they only showed us waves and cliffs on tiny bits of paper.

My reverie was broken when Doris yelled, "Look out!"

She saved me from a small disaster with a pile of sheep manure.

When we started up through the meadow, I had said, "What a pretty sight with all these sheep on the hillside."

"Where there's sheep there's bound to be sheep-heaps," was her reply.

She was right again. Little heaps of dung were everywhere. We climbed through a fence into another pasture and, with some difficulty, found the upper gate that led out into open areas above the pastures, sheep, and sheep-heaps. We soon reached the top of the ridge, and checked the time. It had taken us over thirty minutes to get this far.

"She must be a very fast walker," Doris said, referring to the lady at the farmhouse.

"Yes, but she knows the direct route. And she probably wears boots and doesn't mind what she walks through."

At the top of the ridge we saw way off to our left another slightly higher ridge jutting out into the ocean. On top was what appeared to be some ruins, but it was too far to see them clearly.

"That can't be it; it's too far away. Besides, a castle would have to be bigger ruins than that," I said.

Doris agreed. We started down the other side of the ridge and suddenly the castle appeared in view, right in front of us.

"Good grief," I said, "it's bigger than I thought it would be, and not too ruined either. Come on, let's get down there."

As we got closer, I saw that the walls and towers had been braced with wood poles in an attempt to keep them standing. The towers were perforated by a few gaping holes near the top, which had once been windows. The side of the castle facing us had no doors or any other perforations. A solid wall eight feet high extended from the castle to the cliffs on one end and from the castle to a lake on the other end. The walls, lake, and castle formed an integrated barrier to stop entry to the large peninsula beyond the castle.

Doris said, "I'm not going down there; it looks too dangerous. And I don't want you to go in there either."

"Wait a minute, I'm not going to go inside; it looks too dangerous to me too. But we're still pretty far away, and we could get a little closer without any danger," I bargained.

By mutual consent we stopped on the hillside about one hundred feet above the castle and perhaps three hundred feet away. We sat and munched a little food while enjoying the view.

"Look how close the castle has been built to the edge of the cliffs," said Doris. "What wonderful views they must have had. And, see in front, that beautiful lake. Can't you just imagine the ladies with their men friends paddling about in boats on a warm day? But the castle must have been dark inside. There are not too many windows."

"No and not too many doors either. The cliffs in back and the lake in front would make it difficult to attack the castle in those directions. And, the whole complex cuts off the ridge behind, so the only way for the enemy to attack the castle is from where we sit. Actually, it's more like a fortress than a castle."

"It must have been a beautiful sight back then," said Doris. "How old do you think it is?"

"The farm lady said it was built in the early 1100s. That would be just a few years after the Normans conquered England."

"Well, I don't know about that," said Doris. "You're the history expert."

We sat there a few more minutes enjoying the quiet afternoon, the crisp air, and savoring the rare Irish sunshine.

Finally, I got up and said, "Let's go back. It's getting late, and I'm getting cold."

"Okay, let's go," Doris agreed.

I started back up the way we came.

"Wait. Let's not go back the same way we came," said Doris. "It looks like we could just contour around this ridge rather than go up over it."

"Okay, but I'm not sure it will come out where we want to be."

As we turned the corner of the ridge we found a vehicular track that took us directly to the farmhouse and our bikes in about fifteen minutes.

"See," Doris said, "I thought this was the right way. I wasn't sure, but I knew it was over this way somewhere."

I kept quiet, but smiled to myself, because Doris usually doesn't know where she is.

As we started down the driveway toward the road, the farmhouse lady came out from a row of raspberries. We thanked her again for allowing us to visit the castle and indicated to her our interest in seeing some of the historical sights in Ireland. She was very enthusiastic about ruins and described several that were close by. Apparently, she was on a committee for the preservation of local ruins and, by extension, their history.

"Please come back next week," she invited, as if we

were neighbors just down the road. "I'm so sorry I have such little time today, but next week I'll be free to show you several ruins close by."

We thanked her again and left. We cycled up over a couple hills and came to a fork in the road; both forks were signed to Crookhaven, which was where we wanted to go.

"Let's take the left fork. It looks a little shorter on the map"

"No," said Doris, "this right fork looks better; it's more level, and a more traveled road which means it's probably easier and faster biking."

"But I don't want to be biking on a main road with a bunch of traffic."

"Okay, let's go your way then."

In a few hundred feet, we both got off our bikes and started walking, because the hill was too steep for us to ride. We passed a lady working in her front yard and stopped to talk.

"Tis a beautiful day then," she said.

"Yes, it is a beautiful day," we responded.

From what we could gather every day was a beautiful day in Ireland, if it was not raining. Clouds, wind, and cold did not seem to enter into the equation in determining a beautiful day.

"You're from America," she said. "I can tell from your accent. We don't get too many people from your country out here on bikes."

"We thought biking would be the best way to see Ireland up close," said Doris. "It's so beautiful here."

"Right you are," she said. "You know, I have a sister

who married an American. They live in Boston. I haven't been yet, but I hope to get there later this year."

Among other things, she told us that the road we were on wandered about a bit over hilly country. Very beautiful. But the other road was a better way to get to Crookhaven. We thanked her and said goodbye. We turned our bikes downhill and took the right fork. No words were spoken; I wasn't a masochist that wanted to ride up steep hills when a water level route was available, and Doris was not an "I-told-you-so" person. It turned out that we were the only traffic on the flat level road to Crookhaven.

It was a pretty little village with two pubs and a store that was also the post office. Crookhaven sat partway up a protected inlet at the edge of the water. However, the gorgeous view of the inlet was destroyed by a tacky three-story hostel that wasn't even open. We stayed in a private home at the edge of the village with two rooms to let. From our bedroom window we saw the inlet with its calm waters reflecting the far shore in a double image.

"You're from America," the innkeepers noted. "Such a lovely place. We don't get too many Americans here: you're very welcome. Unfortunately, we won't be home this evening. We must go to a benefit dance at the head of the inlet, but why don't you swing by later and join us there?"

We told them that we would be too tired and needed to go to bed early. I think they simply forgot that we were on bicycles, and what was a fifteen-minute drive for them would be a ninety-minute ride in the dark for us.

Our hostess introduced us to a sixteen-year-old German girl who was staying with them. She was learning English and wanted to come to Seattle to see the memorabilia of rock singer Kurt Cobain. She planned to follow in his footsteps and was learning to play the guitar, but Kurt had committed suicide. So, I hoped she wouldn't follow Kurt too closely.

We tried out both pubs when we first arrived in town. The beer was the same, but the food at one was superior. So, for supper we rode back to the second pub to eat dinner. There, we watched the inevitable soccer game on TV, and talked to the local people. Apparently, Crookhaven was the port of entry and departure for Ireland during those terrible years of the great famine. All ships stopped here going to and from the United States. It was hard to believe that this sleepy little village could have ever supported such an important historical function.

The next morning we biked around the inlet and took pictures of Crookhaven, now reflected in the water on the opposite shore. On the way back to the youth hostel in Schull, we passed an ancient rock tomb in a field near the road. It was similar to many others we saw in Ireland. This one was about waist-high with an open end facing the sea. Several flat rocks on three sides had been tilted on edge to support a roof consisting of two very large flat rocks.

"It's hard to believe these rocks have been in place since the Stone Age, four thousand to five thousand years ago." I told Doris. "Tombs like this one were used as pagan ceremonial sites, until Christianity came along in the 800s. And then were used again, as altars, in the 1800s when Catholic priests were not allowed to perform mass in their churches."

"Maybe they'll be used again in the next thousand years," said Doris. Everywhere we went in Ireland was a history lesson. *So much history in such a small place.*

We finally rode into Schull and turned in our bikes at the hostel. The next day bus service was curtailed because it was a Sunday. Rather than sit around waiting for a late afternoon bus to Dingle, we hitched a ride to Skibbereen to catch an earlier bus. The woman who picked us up cheerfully explained that she had been up, partying all night, and was just now driving home.

"I hope you're good at talking," she said. "I need help in staying awake and not drive off the road." *And weren't we lucky she came along?*

Arriving in Dingle, we continued biking through history, both recent and past.

Trekking the Tatras: Slovakia

"Can we stay overnight?" I yelled into the radio-phone at the Tatra National Park station in the resort town of Stary Smokovec.

Back came the faint reply, "We're filled tonight."

"Oh, no," I said. "We've come such a long way."

Immediately the disembodied voice asked, "Do you mind sleeping on the floor? We can supply each of you with a mattress and a blanket."

"Yes," I shouted, "that would be great."

But I lost radio contact before I was sure of a confirmation.

"Well Doris," I asked, "shall we take a chance that we can stay overnight? It's pretty late, so I don't think we can hike up and make it back this afternoon."

"Oh, I'm sure they'll have a place for us," she said. "Let's just go."

"Will this be too hard on your bad hip?" I asked.

"Nah. I never have trouble going up," Doris claimed.

Yeah, but you gotta come down too.

As usual, she waved aside my concerns. Right there, we committed ourselves to about three thousand feet of elevation gain in six miles to get to Chata Zbojnicka, a Slovakian mountain hut.

We put most of the items we carried around with us in a storage locker, and took only a small daypack of essentials for the trek up the mountain; an extra sweater, some food, toothbrush, and water. We started out about an hour after noon, and aside from a few people who passed us going uphill, we had the trail to ourselves.

"Boy, we're slow," I said. "Everybody passes us."

"What did you expect?" asked Doris. "We're in our late sixties, and everyone else is less than half our age. We're doing just fine."

I had trouble adjusting to the debilitation of age. My mind still assumed that I would be first to the top, like before, and no one could ever pass me going uphill.

The trail led past a pretty mountain lake with clear waters, and funneled us into a rocky gorge. Here the trail was narrow, pressed between rocky slopes and cliffs on one side, and a drop-off into a noisy stream on the other. It went up steeply with built-in steps in many places. Around mid-afternoon we began meeting people coming downhill. The few became a torrent, and we no longer exchanged pleasantries. They hogged the trail walking side by side, forcing us to step off the path on the downhill side to keep from getting run over. Not too nice.

"What's the matter with these people?" I asked. "Can't they walk in single file? There's plenty of room to pass if they did."

"Maybe they're not experienced hikers," said Doris, "more used to sidewalks than walking on trails."

We finally came in sight of the *chata,* the mountain hut, still above us set in a small basin with steep rocky ridges and peaks surrounding it on three sides. Many people were still there strewn about the hut, sitting on rocks in the sun, talking in clumps here and there, and getting ready to plunge *en masse* down the trail. I had no idea so many people hiked the trails in Slovakia.

The hut, built of natural rock and wood, stood among a field of boulders and slabs. Little clumps of vegetation eked out an existence in protected cracks and crevices in the rocky landscape. About fifty feet to one side was a smaller stone building which housed separate bathrooms for men and women. They each had showers and running water, fed by a pure, icy mountain stream. A person would have to be really nasty dirty to brave a shower in that frigid water. We made a stop there before checking in with the hut master, a cute young woman in her mid-twenties.

"Oh, you're the people who called to stay overnight," she said in a lilting, delightful accent as she entered our names in her book. "Our dorm is completely full, but you can sleep on the dining room floor with the other guests who have no beds."

The cost was five hundred SK, about ten dollars, and didn't include food or drinks. Nor did she mention a mattress and blanket for the night. Beyond the office we passed the dorm, a room about twenty-by-thirty feet jammed with sixteen bunks.

"Maybe we were lucky not to get a bed," said Doris, shaking her head at the crowded, closed-in space.

The main room was the dining room filled with long tables and benches. Across one end was the kitchen closed-off from the dining room except for a pass-through opening for dispensing food.

"Look at all the people eating soup," I said. "It must be pretty good stuff. You want to try some?"

"Sure," said Doris, "but why don't you find out what kind of soup it is first? I don't want to be slurping a greasy broth with some kind of strange meat floating around in it."

I asked, but the name was unpronounceable Slovakian. So, I got some to try anyway. It was made from red cabbage, slightly sour, and absolutely delicious. We had seconds, and I was thinking about thirds, but Doris, ever practical, reminded me that suppertime was just around the corner.

We went out, and strolled about the hut to see the rugged, rocky mountains and ridges surrounding us. The hut was already in shadow and, without the sun, the air was chilly. Almost everyone not staying overnight had left for the comfort of the flatlands below, and the number of people left behind was more manageable. A breeze started blowing, making the late afternoon downright cold. We found a place on some warm rocks out of the wind, and watched the shadows rise toward the rocky summits around us as the sun, out of our sight, got lower in the sky. We talked briefly with a Polish couple and then with some Germans who had spent time in America. They spoke good English and wanted us to sit with them at supper.

We met Mark, a young man in his mid-twenties. He was the only other American staying at the hut, and he sat with us until time to go in. We had fun hearing American spoken with all the idioms and slang words which were so little understood in the rest of the world. He was working in Krakow, Poland, designing logos for tee shirts. His specialty was working English words not readily understood in Poland into the designs. His command of the American language was perfect for that job. He pointed out a trail still visible in the sunlight that came down off a ridge above us.

"That's a one-way trail," he said.

"What do you mean, *one-way trail?* I've never heard of such a thing," I said.

"Well, they have them here in the Tatras. It's because the terrain is so rough. They put in fixed chains and ladders and things like that for safety. You probably wouldn't want to meet another party halfway up a ladder coming from the opposite direction."

"How do you know which trail is one-way?" I asked.

"They're marked on the map. Each trail is color-coded and that color is painted on rocks along the way in dashes or dots of the proper color. One-way trails have arrows pointing the right direction."

"Why don't they just go around such rough places to make the trail easier and safer?"

"I don't know," said Mark. "Maybe, because it's more fun."

More fun? Since when does fun take precedence over safety? Certainly not in the States, I thought.

Just then, someone announced that supper was ready, and we scurried into the dining room along with everyone else still outside We sat at the table with Mark and the German couple as the kitchen staff ladled out generous portions of food: potatoes, the inevitable pork, cabbage, and soup. I hoped the soup would be the same as what we had earlier, but the cooks had varied the menu to a namby-pamby vegetable soup. Too bad. We bought a bottle of wine along with just about everyone else, so our table was not lacking for wine. However, the mountain hut style of drinking was very restrained, and a bottle for two lasted all evening.

The noise in the dining room was a cacophony of sound that came from people talking in a Babel of languages. After supper some people played cards, but we, like most everyone else, sat and talked, told stories, and laughed a lot. Shortly after the kitchen crew had finished their clean-up, the hut manager announced the time for lights out; ten o'clock p.m., when the generator would be shut down for the night.

Almost immediately, we lost our table and bench. In a flurry of action, the young people moved all the tables to one end of the dining room, and stacked the benches on top. Their big packs suddenly appeared and out of them came foam pads and sleeping bags, and a lot of other stuff. We managed to snag a favorable spot against one wall for our sleeping area, head to the wall and feet toward the center of the room. These places were finite, because of the limited amount of walls. They were in demand, because any place in the center of the room was prone to others walking through that space and stumbling over bodies, especially in the dark. We prepared to make do with sleeping directly on the floor with our daypacks as pillows.

Just then, one of the hut employees entered and asked loudly, "Where are the older people who don't have pads or sleeping bags? Are they here? I have mattresses and blankets for them."

Those older people were Doris and me, of course. They hadn't forgotten us, but I wished they could have been a little more discreet in making their announcement. Each mattress was just wide enough for a single body and only a little thicker than a foam pad. It was a great improvement from the bare floor, and fine for me. But Doris always had trouble with her bony hips poking into the ground, or, in this case, the hard floor. On camping trips she carried a second piece of foam material to pad her hips. That night she improvised using a sweater. We each got a scratchy wool blanket, but still used our packs for pillows. I slept like a rock.

Before bedding down, Doris and I made one last trip out into the cold night to the bathroom. She informed me later that she counted twenty-six bodies in the dining room, two in the hallway, and four outside in the cold. Brrr. This was plus the thirty-two allegedly bunking in the overcrowded dorm, which Doris declined to enter and count. Adding in the staff, our *chata* was a substantial village.

I lay awake for a while after the lights went out listening to low voices, whispers, the occasional laugh, and shuffling noises as people settled down to sleep. What took Doris and me two minutes to do seemed to take these young people hours. Next to us two young men settled in and then started giggling. I never heard men giggle before, and was fascinated until I finally got tired of hearing it. I went to sleep before the room was completely quiet. During the night I woke up a couple times to hear shuffling noises of people moving about, snores, coughs, groans, and other bodily noises before I zonked-off to sleep again.

The next morning we ate breakfast with Mark, who had spent a miserable night in the dorm.

"It was too stuffy and noisy in there," he said. "Just too many people crammed into a little space."

He and his Polish friends were taking the trail up over the ridge in back of the hut, and then dropping down to hike into Poland and travel back to Krakow.

"I would love to go up to that ridge," I told him, "but it looks like a long way up and back. And we'd still have to get to Stary Smokovec to catch our train out."

"You don't have to come back here," he said showing me his map. "See, from that ridge the trail leads across a small valley, and up to a second ridge. From there my friends and I turn toward Poland, but you could follow a one-way trail that takes you back to town."

"That would make a great loop trip," I said, as I traced the route on the map with my finger. "And we could find out about one-way trails. Neat."

Inside I was jumping with excitement.

"What do you think?" I asked Doris.

"Sure," she said, "let's do it."

It was an answer I'd come to expect, and fifteen minutes

later we were on our way. Mark gave us his map, because as he said, "I'm going home and don't need it anymore." The trail soon deteriorated to simply scrambling up over rocks following little blue dots painted to show the way along a non-existent trail. The ridge was over 1,300 feet above the *chata,* and the route became steeper the higher we got. Part way up, Mark caught up to us, and climbed with us a little way. We were pretty slow, so he finally went on ahead. I thought we might not see him again, but when we reached the top of the ridge, he was sitting comfortably with his back against a rock writing in a notebook.

"The easy part is over," he said, as he jerked his head in the direction of a notch we had to pass through.

Doris took one look at the other side and gasped, "it's straight down. We can't go down this cliff."

I didn't say anything, but mentally agreed.

"We don't go down yet," I said. "See the chain to our right leading across the face of the cliff. You can see that it ends at a fixed rope that drops down to the top of that gully. I can't see any further, but there must be something else to help us get down. This is supposed to be a trail."

"Some trail," said Doris. "You go first."

I grabbed the chain and crabbed my way out on the rock face. Surprisingly, I found lots of hidden crevices and knobs for my Tevas. I only take these sandals on our trips, so whatever terrain I'm on, they have to suffice. Fortunately, the traverse was short, about two-hundred feet, and was easier than it looked. Looking back, I saw

Mark watching my progress. I don't know if he knew about this obstacle. He never said.

When I reached the rope and grabbed it, Doris let out a yell, "Wait for me. Don't you dare go down that rope until I catch up."

I waited and encouraged her across the face of the cliff, suggesting possible places for her feet. She had a little trouble because her size twelve shoes were so big they wouldn't fit into some of the crevices I had used. But she did fine, and had a big grin on her face when she caught up. *She's sure a gutsy woman,* I thought.

I gripped the rope hard, and went down the cliff backwards. The rock was broken-up a little, and marginally less steep than the rock face back at the notch. The rope extended a little further down out of sight into a gully, but I waited at the bottom of the cliff for Doris to come down and join me. She clung to the rope for dear life, talking and cursing to herself all the way down.

When she joined me I got a big hug and a kiss.

"Isn't this fun?" she exclaimed.

Then she saw the steep gully below our feet with no helpful ropes, no chains, no nothing, just a gut-wrenching steep slope of loose rocks and scree ending at a trail way down below.

"Oh my god," she wailed, "What'll we do now?"

"We go down very carefully," I responded. "Just ask yourself, what's the worst thing that can happen?"

"I'll slip and fall to my death," she replied.

"No way, if you slip, you'll just slide down on your butt on a bunch of loose rock and stop on that trail down below. You may have a few bruises on your rear end, but that's pretty well padded."

"Very funny," she said, as she started down, sliding and balancing on the loose rocks and scree as she went.

She managed to get down with only a couple bumps on her rear end while I ended up on my butt several times getting off that miserable slope the Slovakians called a trail. Looking up the way we came, Mark and his friends were starting down. So, we moved away on the trail to get out of the fall line of any rocks they might dislodge. Such a rock could funnel into the gully, bounce into the air, and come whirling down on our heads. Loose airborne rocks made a terrifying whizzing sound as they came at you, and even a rock the size of a golf ball had been known to break an arm.

The trail contoured around the upper part of a small valley, through some stunted low bushes and sparse grass with a spindly flower or two. It crossed several small streams, and we felt like we were in a paradise after spending the morning on bleak rock. Mark and his friends caught up and passed us where the trail started back up through a steep rock fall to the second ridge. We clawed and scrambled up over boulders, the route marked for us with the ubiquitous blue dots. When we got to the top Mark and his friends greeted us again. We took pictures and traded hugs like old friends before saying a final goodbye. They went down toward Poland and we went down the opposite direction to catch the train at Stary Smokovec.

Now, we followed little blue arrows painted on the

rocks indicating the direction of travel on a one-way trail. We scrambled across two more rock faces holding on to chains embedded in the rock, and descended two ladders before getting off that second ridge. The trail became less steep, and we entered a broad, beautiful meadow-like valley, very green, with short-cropped grass. In several places flagstones paved the trail, like a sidewalk.

"This is disappointing," I said. "There's no reason for a one-way trail here."

"There sure was, back near the top of the ridge," said Doris.

"Not really. People could easily wait their turn to pass those obstacles. They were short distances and completely open to view."

We entered thick woods, and other hikers passed us, some with little children, all looking forward to having some fun on this trail. The trail looked nondescript to us, just a normal well-traveled path through the woods. Ordinary, that is, until we were cliffed-out forty feet above a river.

The trail stopped abruptly at a cliff; nowhere to go. I was puzzled until I saw the first of many small steel grates projecting from the vertical face of the rock walls. They reminded me of snowshoes whimsically embedded in solid rock, and they extended across the face of the cliff for as far as I could see.

"Oh what fun," said Doris. "We have to go around the cliff on those cute little grates. How exciting."

The authorities had fastened a chain at chest height to grab onto for safety. Great. We slowly crabbed our way out on the surface of the cliff hanging on to the chain for dear life. Each grate was large enough to rest both feet, and the gap between the grates was mercifully small. We had unobstructed views down through the open grates of the raging torrent of water forty feet below. With sweaty palms and adrenaline pumping through my veins, I became an ardent cliff hugger.

"Don't look down," I said. "It's not so scary."

"But then I can't see where my feet are going. I might miss a grate," she said, hanging on to the chain in a white knuckled grip.

"I mean don't look beyond your feet, past the grate," I said. "Just ignore all that white rushing water and rocks."

"Are you kidding? That's like trying to ignore a semi passing you at eighty miles an hour. I just hope the guys who set these grates knew what they were doing."

The grates went around several bends, and after getting over the initial rush of fear, I relaxed a little and enjoyed the experience. The grates ended in about four hundred feet where a normal trail led us off into the woods. How boring. The exciting part was over too soon.

"Can you imagine a family with little kids going around that cliff on those grates?" asked Doris.

"Not hardly," I replied. "But can you imagine meeting a bunch of people half way across, coming from the opposite direction? Now I know why they have one-way trails."

"I hope we find other exciting places," said Doris.

We did encounter other grated spots, and had to climb

long ladders without hand rails set next to waterfalls, or up steep cliff faces, but nothing as scary and exciting as that first set of grates. I don't know how parents got their children over these obstacles, but this was family fun in Slovakia.

When the trail became a two-way route again, we met a lot more hikers, and finally reached Slienzsky Dom, a large two-story hotel and restaurant. Large groups of people moved about in a frenzy of activity, much like a disturbed beehive. And of all things, we saw cars and parking lots where no such things ought to be.

We looked around the hotel while making disparaging remarks about the trappings of civilization in such a beautiful and remote setting. We rested and tried to relax while eating a bowl of soup in the crowded, noisy dining room.

"Do you want to try to get a ride back?" I asked, before starting on.

"No way," said Doris, "I want to get away from this place and back on the trail."

By now we had been hiking and scrambling for about six hours, so I knew Doris was starting to hurt. She needed a hip replacement, but was putting it off until she really got old, or until it hurt too badly. She never said much about it, just gritted her teeth and went on. I could always tell when she hurt, because we hiked slower and slower. She even tried walking backwards to relieve the pain. I tried to help by picking out the easiest way around roots and obstructions in the trail. But, the last few miles were hell for her, and her cheerful, sunny disposition was buried in pain.

Doris stays on a Slovakian trail by following the colored dots.

Doris navigates a trail of steel grates.

When we reached Stary Smokovec we found a place to sit in a crowded eatery. Doris recovered a little, while eating a bratwurst sandwich with sauerkraut. She shared a second one with me, ate a giant side of German potato salad, drank a bottle of beer, and then ate the bigger half of our apple strudel. She quickly emerged from under her cloud of discomfort caused by her worn out hip and cheerfully joined me in catching the train onward to our next adventure.

A Party for Shiva: India

A procession stopped us from crossing a street on a warm sticky evening in Ernaculam in the State of Kerala, India. Fascinated, Doris and I watched two priests lead a group of people carrying candles and chanting a mantra in a continuous monotone. The priests moved about calling out and waving their arms to exhort their followers to continue chanting. They were barefoot and bare to the waist, each wearing a bright flower-patterned wraparound skirt tucked in at the waist. Their skin glistened with sweat as if oiled. The sweat collected in beads to form rivulets, running down their chests and across their great, bronzed, bare bellies.

Men, women, and children shuffled along behind the priests raising dust that hung in the still air of early evening. They wore necklaces of marigold blossoms, whose bright golden blossoms contrasted beautifully with the marchers' light brown skin. The pungent smell of marigolds mixed with the odor of burning candles permeated the air, masking those other smells of India; spices, garbage, and animal dung.

The women looked so graceful in their colorful *saris*. Red ribbons fluttered from the single braid down the center of their back, and many multicolored bracelets covered their arms. They wore ankle bracelets that jingled when they walked, and long earrings that sparkled in the dark. The procession was accompanied by a few musicians rapping a staccato beat on tambourines, accompanied by the jingle of tiny cymbals. One instrument emitted querulous reedy sounds that to my Western ears sounded unmusical, and it went on forever without break. The procession had traffic backed up for blocks behind it, but no one seemed to mind. We watched for a while, mesmerized by the color, the music, and the strong smell of marigolds.

Later, in our hotel room after supper, I opened the window and heard the same music or at least similar music coming from someplace nearby. The sky lit up occasionally with fireworks, great bursts of bright green, scarlet and yellow in the shape of giant balls, shooting stars, and curtains of falling color, punctuated by ear-splitting booms of exploding aerial bombs. Not far away, I heard muffled voices made by crowds of people. It all seemed so exciting that I persuaded Doris to go with me to investigate.

"What's going on with all that noise outside?" I asked the hotel clerk standing behind his counter.

He answered in that delightful lilting inflection that many Indians have when speaking English. "Oh sir, it is Shiva. He has come to live in the temple. It is a large celebration for he is a very important god."

"So, that's what the procession we saw was all about, I said. "Can anyone go to see the festival?

"Oh yes, most assuredly. Everyone is welcome."

"What time do they close down? I mean, will we have time to see anything if we go out now?"

"The temple will not close tonight. The celebration goes on night and day. It will not stop for five days; you will see."

I couldn't help being a little incredulous and said with a smile, "Well, at least the music will have to stop when the players get tired."

"Oh my, no," he said, raising his hands in protest and shaking his head vigorously. "That would never do. The music is most important, and must continue night and day for five days. That is prescribed in the celebration to Shiva. Many musicians are waiting to take the place of those who become tired."

"We better start learning to like this music if it's going to be around that long," I muttered to Doris as we left the hotel.

"Hey, what don't you like?" asked Doris. "Its beat is steady and throbbing, like those wonderful boom boxes at home."

"Yeah, great. And maybe that reedy sounding music is better than our squealing electric guitars, too."

I knew that in the pantheon of Hindu gods, the three at the top were Brahma, Shiva and Vishnu. I also knew they were far more real to the Indian people than our abstract idea of God, Christ, and the Holy Spirit. Their gods married and had children, and on occasion reinvented themselves as new gods; manifestations of their original selves. Their emotions ran the gamut of love, anger, jealousy and all the other feelings of mankind.

I thought Shiva was perhaps the most interesting of all the gods. He gave life and he took life. He was the creator of heaven and earth. He was depicted dancing on one foot with the other raised, for if ever both feet touched the ground the world would end. He was usually shown dancing on the back of a demon. The demon represented ignorance of the gods, and forgetfulness of the gods. I figured that pretty well covered any excuses for not relating to a god.

He was also a god of contradictions. On one hand, he was the greatest lover of all time, married to the extremely beautiful and sexy goddess, Parvati. His sexual exploits were legendary and his easily recognized phallic symbol, the *lingam*, was worshipped everywhere in India.

I mentioned this to Doris, but she remained unimpressed.

"You men'll go to any extent to promote the importance of a penis," was her response.

"But he's also considered to be the greatest ascetic of all time," I said. "The ideas of abstinence and yoga came from him, and from the power of his concentration in meditation, he's able to create whatever man can imagine."

"What are you talking about?" asked Doris, "and what's this got to do with his *lingam?*"

I went on to tell Doris about how Parvati hated Shiva's

renowned powers of concentration, because he tuned her out and paid no attention to her, refusing her sexual overtures while he was thinking his great thoughts.

"Well," said Doris, "that sounds like somebody I know, and he's standing right beside me."

I didn't reply to that and went on.

"Parvati finally got so mad at Shiva that she sent their son Kama to shoot him with an arrow of desire, just like a cupid. Desire brought Shiva out of his meditation all right, but he was so teed-off that he burned up the messenger, his own son. Burned him up, dead."

"I would have shot him with an arrow, period. Forget the part about desire," said Doris.

"Wait, there's more. During their lengthy lovemaking, Parvati persuaded Shiva to bring their son back to life. He finally agreed to do it, but only on the condition that he would give his son the head of the first animal he saw. This happened to be an elephant and that's how the god, Gnash, came into being, a man's body with an elephant head."

"Oh, he's cute. I've seen little statues of him everywhere."

"He's known as the god of prosperity and good luck," I went on, "and everyone likes him."

As we walked along the night air was a little cooler, a pleasant softly warm temperature. We followed the noises of music and people's voices until we came to an enclosure surrounding a temple. The people were laughing and talking in a holiday mood, and they meandered about drifting in and out of the open gates to the temple grounds. Blue, red, green, and yellow neon lights lit up the night, and as we walked forward several colorful rockets burst overhead accompanied by ear-splitting aerial bombs. Outside the temple enclosure, booths served fast food, souvenirs, and offered games of chance, just like a county fair at home.

We wandered into the temple grounds, and gaudy neon lights assaulted us from all sides; on temple walls, poles, trees, and strung on wires in midair. In the dark the wires were hard to see, so strips of bright colors appeared to be floating haphazardly in midair. Continuous music with the beat of drums provided an insidious background noise to the voices and laughter of the Indian families who wandered about.

An elephant covered with beautiful embroidered blankets and bedecked with large costume jewelry attracted many people. With his dexterous trunk he plucked rupees from any volunteer with a rupee to spare. He took it out of their hand, or pocket, or just about anywhere the end of his trunk could manage to intrude. Like two fat fingers at the end of his trunk he picked up and held the relatively small coin and then carefully deposited it into a slot in a box nearby. The volunteer never got his rupee back.

We walked into the temple, but the action there was minimal. Shiva had already been removed to his bedroom. He went to bed every night in a solemn ceremony with priests carrying his statue from his daytime altar to a room set aside for him only. Occasionally a statue of Parvati shared the bedroom. There he rested, ate, and meditated until morning, when the priests arrived to carry him back to officiate at his altar, again.

In another part of the temple a few women prayed to their patron goddess, Khali, who they considered to be the divine mother representing the strong maternal bond between mother and child. However, she was also a ferocious goddess originally sent to slay a demon that threatened the destruction of the world. She carried a sword and the severed head of the demon in two of her four hands, and was naked except for a girdle made of men's arms with hands attached and a garland of many skulls thrown over her shoulders. The women bought small pieces of butter furnished by the priests to throw on her fearsome and intimidating statue. In that way, they hoped to mellow her out a little to hear their prayers. As a consequence, Khali was barely recognizable under accumulated layers of rancid butter.

"See there," I said, "the Indian ladies butter up their goddess to get what they want."

"Not just Khali," said Doris. "We women have buttered up you men for years to get what we need."

We finally found the source of the music. It came from four musicians sitting on a makeshift stage on one side of the temple playing two drums, a guitar-like instrument, and the inevitable querulous reed instrument. The music wasn't entirely unpleasant, just strange, and I think the familiar sounds from the guitar player helped make it more pleasing. Many people including family groups sat on the grass in front of the stage listening. Contrary to the information I received, the music did stop, but only for seconds at a time. During one of those brief pauses some ladies came out on the stage to dance and the strangeness of the music no longer mattered.

Doris decided that dancing ladies were not too interesting, and gathering a few rupees from me, went off to play with the elephant.

The women danced barefoot, dressed in long tight skirts of monochrome red. They wore short-sleeved, tight-fitting, bodices of one color; bright green or yellow. They were beautiful women, full-bodied, their faces highly made up. The tight skirts confined them to using small steps for moving about in their dances. Most of the action was with arms, hands, and fingers with long painted nails forming stylized gestures which the audience seemed to understand. Although, I didn't understand the story of the dance, I certainly enjoyed its gracefulness and the beauty of the women.

The dances went on for a long time, long enough for my legs to alternately cramp up, or become numb. Still, I waited for the one dance I wanted to see. I saw it only once before when I was in Northern India ten years before. This was Southern India, so it might not be performed here. Finally, a dancer came out alone carrying a shallow metal bowl rounded on the bottom and about eighteen inches in diameter. I heard murmurs and rustling in the crowd watching. I knew she would perform the dance I wanted to see, and apparently the audience knew it too.

She placed the bowl on the stage floor where it gently rocked on its rounded bottom. Then she placed her bare feet on the rim of the bowl and balanced herself there.

I don't know how she managed to get her feet placed on the edge of the bowl without falling off. When the music started, she began moving the bowl about the stage without moving her feet. By swaying and maneuvering her bodyweight she guided herself and the bowl about the stage wherever she desired. She glided across the floor almost effortlessly with the most sinuous and graceful movements. At the same time, her arms and hands told the story of the dance, but I was fascinated with the movements of her body and the incredible balance required of her to stay on the rim of a bowl.

Like the end of any show, the bowl dance was the climax of the dancing for that period of time. Most of the audience sitting on the grass left after it was finished. I also got up to leave, hobbling along until my legs recovered from sitting cross-legged for so long. The crowds of people had thinned, but still the music pressed on and occasional rockets and bombs punctuated the velvety night. I picked up Doris who by now had lost all her rupees to that insatiable elephant. We left the temple grounds by the main entrance opposite from where we had entered, and walked down a broad walkway lined with shade trees brightly lit-up with neon lights for Shiva and the people he attracted.

The walkway ended at a main street across from a large park. Folding chairs sat in straight orderly rows filled with people listening to an outdoor Christian service. Over in the direction of Shiva's temple I heard shouts and laughter. But here, the service was conducted quietly and decorously in two languages by two men. One spoke first in English, and then the other in Malayalam, the language of the State of Kerala. I assumed it was the same sermon. Meanwhile, Shiva's colorful rocket bursts failed to interrupt the service. At last, a malicious flurry of aerial bombs sounding like immense claps of thunder obliterated the final words of the preachers. Shiva apparently knew the best time to try to disrupt the Christian service.

But, it didn't work. The ministers simply repeated themselves and their service ended as decorously as it had been conducted. Yet, if I were a man ignorant of religion, and given a choice of the two great religions offered that night; I might be tempted to choose the bright lights, dancing women, fireworks, performing elephants, and music that never stopped.

Travel Angels:
Czech Republic

Doris loves angels. I'm sure she likes those heavenly ones we can't see. *Don't we all?* But, it's those angelic minions, replicas found in gift shops all over the world that she likes too. As a result she filled our house with little angels that peer at me in every room from shelves, tables, windowsills, and even the bathroom where one watches me wash my hands every day. I swear one or two have waved a wing at me when I've been unusually angelic, which is not too often.

These angels have two things in common: they're all female, and they all have wings. So, I find it hard to go along with Doris when she identifies a male stranger, without wings, as an angel. It's a little easier for me when she points out a female as an angel. Aren't they all in some way?

She calls them travel angels, and they usually help us at difficult times. No matter how much we learn about a country—the language, and the culture, we still need to ask for help to get around independently. Fortunately, most people react positively to the word "help," otherwise many of us "independent travelers" would have difficulty flitting about the world on our own.

Doris has standards for her travel angels. It's not enough just to respond to a question or be helpful in some way. Those are merely nice people, and they are almost universal. Her travel angels earn their wings by stopping to listen, spending the time to understand our broken language, and going the extra mile to help us out. They never ask for anything in return, and are usually well-disguised. Sometimes, she doesn't recognize angels until much later, too late to give them the thanks and gratitude they deserve.

I always agreed with her assessment of the people she terms as angels, but I never designated a person as a travel angel myself until the day we arrived to change trains in Brn, Czech Republic. I bought the tickets, and remembered to ask what track the train was on, number six, and at what time it would depart. With all bases covered and still a half an hour to go before the train left, I talked Doris into joining me for a beer in the station pub. After all, this was Czech Republic, home of the famous Pilsner beer. At fifteen minutes before the train left, we sauntered out onto the platform through the great glass doors, where we easily found tracks seven through twenty-four designated by large numbered signs.

"Where are tracks one through six?" I asked Doris, not really expecting her to know.

Frantically, I asked the people around us. No one knew, or they didn't understand me. We ran back to the ticket agent's cage, and got in line. We now had ten minutes left, and Doris was mumbling something about guzzling beer at the wrong time. I was next in line, but a little stout lady in front of me blocked the entire window engaged in a long-winded discussion with the ticket agent.

Finally, in desperation I turned to the six or seven people behind us in line, and in a firm, calm voice asked in English, "Excuse me, pardon me. Where is track six?"

I probably said more, and probably not so calmly, but I don't remember. A couple of people smiled, and a couple of others looked away embarrassed for me. That was the total response. The lady in front of me finally moved off, and I turned back to the ticket agent.

Just then I felt someone tapping me on the arm. I jerked around with a scowl, because I don't like strangers touching me. A seedy, non-descript little man perhaps five feet tall who was standing in line behind us had reached around Doris to get my attention. I dismissed him and turned my attention to the ticket agent.

"Where is track six," and I showed him my tickets.

He explained in Czech waving his arms toward the platform. I shook my head. He drew a map and shoved it at me. A few steps away, I tried to read the map, but I couldn't figure it out. With only a few minutes left before the train departed, I knew the map was useless. The little man who had bothered me before had left his place in line, and was now standing in front of me tugging at my arm again.

He wore a dirty orange shirt and baggy pants. His

face behind a few days stubble of a beard crinkled in a mass of wrinkles from a wide smile. He was missing front teeth, so his grin had a gaping black hole in the middle of it.

He held up six fingers and said, "Seecks."

"Where?" I asked.

He motioned us toward track platforms seven through twenty-four.

"Doris, we don't have time to try anything else, let's go. Maybe he does know where to go, but we're going to have to run for it and hope the train is late."

We followed the little man through the great glass doors onto the track platform. By now we were running. At the end of the platform we stepped down to the ground and turned the corner of the station. Beyond were sidings with long rows of rusting coaches sitting in storage. The man continued to trot along a path in the weeds around the ends of the old coaches. No track six here, and with nothing else we could do, we continue to follow the little man. Suddenly, we rounded a high chain link fence, and miraculously came to the missing tracks, one through six, with a train on track six. Our little guide was talking to a train official by the time we caught up. It was our train, and he motioned us on.

We passed through several coaches to find an empty compartment. Settling in, we looked out the window and there was our guide waving to us with that big grin on his face. I opened the window and we shouted our thanks. And Doris blew him a kiss or two. Suddenly his face got serious. He pursed his lips and wrinkled up his forehead in concentration before he spoke.

"Ray-mam-beer Burn, ees gooot."

Just then the train whistle let loose and the train moved forward cutting off any more attempts at conversation. The last we saw of him was his big toothless grin and waving arms.

"That's definitely an angel, first class," I exclaimed, "with a wonderfully good disguise."

"Yes," Doris agreed, "and remember, Brn is good."

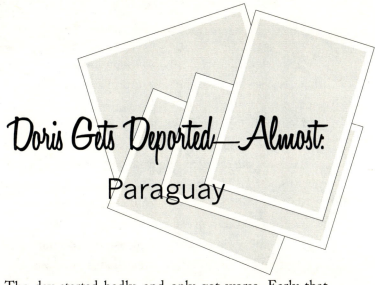

Doris Gets Deported—Almost:
Paraguay

The day started badly, and only got worse. Early that morning we bussed our way from Falls Iguazu, Argentina to Paraguay. On the way we had to cross a small sliver of Brazil lying between those countries. The trick was to get our passports stamped out of Argentina at the border of Brazil, and then wait for an international bus to Paraguay, thereby skipping through Brazil without having to stop for their border formalities.

A visitor's visa for Brazil cost a whopping sixty-four dollars per person, and had kept us from going there in the first place. We viewed the Iguazu Falls from the Argentina side instead of seeing them from Brazil. Of course, we kept getting reports that the falls looked better from the Brazilian side, kind of like the grass is always greener somewhere else.

We entered Paraguay in a traffic jam through the center of Ciudad Del Este (City of the East,) not able to tell where Brazil left off and Paraguay began. But after going several blocks I broke the news to Doris.

"I think we've passed the immigration and customs office. It's no big deal, but we're probably in Paraguay illegally."

I said this with half a smile on my face, but she was not amused.

"What?" she cried, raising both arms in alarm. "Why didn't they stop? We've got to go back before they put us in jail."

Doris sometimes overstates minor problems.

"We're okay right now as long as we're on the bus," I said, trying to calm her down, although that was like trying to calm a whirlwind.

"Well, we can't spend the rest of lives riding around on this bus," she responded "We've got to get off and go back."

"Not now. Let's get to the bus station so we know where we are. It can't be very far away now. Once we're there we can figure out what to do."

At the bus terminal located at the edge of the city we put our packs in storage, and bought onward tickets to the capital, Asuncion. The bus left late in the afternoon, so we had plenty of time to solve our immigration problem. We took a local bus back into the city center, and got off when I judged we were close to the immigration and customs office. There, we got our passports stamped and became legal again, although the custom guys never had a chance to look at our packs stored back at the bus station.

"We have time before our bus leaves," I said. "Let's go out to see the dam."

"What dam?" asked Doris.

"The Itaipu Dam. I told you all about it before, don't you remember? It's the biggest dam in the world."

I have a thing for dams and try to see them all if Doris doesn't object too much. She generally goes along, but she just isn't into dams. I don't know why.

"Oh, that dam," she said. "You mean its close enough to see from here?"

"According to the map it's a little north of town," I said, "and the guidebook tells us where to catch the bus to get out there."

"Can we walk to the bus stop?" asked Doris. "I hate to take a taxi."

"Me too," I said. "I think it's only a half mile or so to walk."

So we started walking through the city. Shops spilled their wares into the sidewalk selling everything under the sun, but mainly electronic goods that were apparently cheaper at this border town than in Brazil or Argentina. We never saw a price tag and even had to bargain to buy a Coke along the way.

We pushed through crowds of people buying up shoes, clothing apparel, cell phones, computer parts, and video games. Sidewalks disappeared under mounds of merchandise, forcing us to detour into the street to get around. We sweltered in the mid-morning heat, and grimly bore the noise and confusion of the traffic. Crowds of people clogged our way, shoving and bargaining in loud voices. Sweat ran off my forehead and down my nose, and I felt it trickling down under my clothes.

Away from the city center the sidewalk ended and we used a pathway beside the busy street. We went through an area that looked like a solid waste landfill with newspaper, plastic bags, and debris scattered in the weeds and sparse grass. Piles of smelly garbage lay rotting in the heat across our path, forcing us to walk in the street around them. The heat and the odors got worse. The heavy traffic got more dangerous as drivers speeded along, free of the jams back in town.

At a gas station, Doris insisted that I ask where we were. She believed that gas stations the world over were put on earth to dispense directions as well as gas. I hated to ask directions, especially at a gas station. Doris says it's a "man thing."

"I already know where we are. We're on Avenidas San Blas. See the sign on the street? Right there in front of you."

"I've seen those signs all along the way," said Doris, "so I know what street we're on. But how far do we have to walk to catch the bus? We've gone more than a half mile."

I think both of us were sagging under the brutal heat. A large thermometer on the side of the gas station registered forty three degrees centigrade, which I computed to be about 110 degrees Fahrenheit. So, when the man I asked about directions offered us a ride in his pick-up, we accepted, even though he was only going a few blocks toward our destination. We hopped in the back for the short, bumpy ride. When he dropped us off, fate intervened by placing an empty taxi at that exact spot in the world. Doris and I looked at each other and without words went over to bargain with the driver for a ride to our bus stop. He was sitting in the shade of a small tree, the doors of his taxi wide open. At first he seemed a little reluctant to go such a short distance, but we finally agreed to a price of three mil. That meant three thousand guarani in Paraguay currency, or about $1.50. What a relief to ride in the heat instead of walking in it!

At the bus stop the driver held up three fingers, and said in pretty clear English, "Three dollars."

"What? No way, the price was three mil guarani," I said, pulling the money from my pocket.

"No, no," he said in a loud voice pushing the money I offered away with disdain. "Only dollars. Three."

We objected, and the driver began to yell. Soon a knot of people surrounded us like a crowd at a cockfight. They were talking and yelling too, maybe even laying bets. In the circle were Doris and I, the rich Americans on one side pitted against the poor itinerant taxi driver on the other. All because of an extra $1.50. How embarrassing!

The noise finally drew the attention of a policeman who listened to the driver speaking in eloquent Spanish, and then to our broken baby Spanish. Maybe, it was the crowd around us that persuaded the policeman to rule in our favor, or maybe he didn't like taxi drivers either, but whatever the reason, we were ordered to pay the man the agreed fare of G3000. Just then our bus came along. I quickly paid the belligerent driver, and we jumped aboard the bus before he could protest any further, or the policeman could change his mind.

"No more taxis," said Doris with a grim look on her face. "They're a rotten, greedy bunch."

"Oh come on, it was only $1.50 extra that he wanted."

"No," said Doris, "it was two times the agreed price."

The bus dropped us off on the main road opposite a guarded gate on a parallel access road that led to the dam site. Beyond was the visitor's center. We wondered why the bus didn't leave us off back down the road where the access road branched off. Now we had to backtrack around a six feet high fence with coiled barbwire on top to enter the dam grounds.

Then I noticed a narrow footpath through the weeds leading down off the road to a small hole cut in the fence. Someone had slashed the wire mesh with a vertical and horizontal cut, and bent the heavy wire back on itself to form enough opening for a person to wiggle through.

"Here's a short cut," I said.

"No way," said Doris. "Those guards will put us in jail for trespassing."

"But people must use this way to get to and from the dam and the bus stop. They wouldn't leave a hole cut in a security fence without a reason."

"Oh yeah they would. Just to trap unwary foreigners and extort money for illegal entry."

"Your brains are frying in the heat," I said. "Come on, let's go to the visitor center. They might have some air conditioning."

We entered the dam grounds, stooping and twisting to get through the hole in the fence. When we walked past the guardhouse, no guards appeared, and the visitor center was closed for lunch. *Maybe the whole damn dam was closed for lunch.* We had a half hour to wait and wandered off to one side of the building to wait in the shade of a tree. Nearby, another building housed the guards while off duty, and we saw a couple of them sitting with their chairs tilted back conversing over Paraguayan music blasting out from a portable radio.

After a minute or so, one of them waved us over to sit with them out of the heat. Their windows were wide open so I couldn't see how the heat would be less inside than outside under our tree. But we went over anyway out of courtesy for their kind offer, and the thought we might antagonize them in some way by refusing. Once inside we felt the wind blowing from fans, and the effect was a little cooler, and we thanked them for that luxury. It was also a relief to know that the armed guards here might be ordinary people.

An hour later the visitor center opened and we inquired about the dam tour which was supposed to have started a half hour before. We noticed many people seated in the waiting area and assumed they were also waiting for a tour to start.

"Oh, you speak English," said the receptionist, a little flustered to have foreigners wanting a tour. "Please wait over there. We have English-speaking guide for you," she said proudly.

"Over there" was across the room from the Spanish-speaking people. Finally they left *en masse*. And still we waited. And waited.

"Why are we waiting?" I whispered to Doris. "Everyone else is gone."

"Cool your jets. Relax," she responded, knowing that patience was not one of my virtues.

Finally, I couldn't stand it any longer and again asked the receptionist about the tour.

"They go," she said in alarm. "Why you still here?"

"You told us to wait for an English-speaking guide."

"Oh, she's over there. I'll get her for you."

"They forgot us," I hissed to Doris, angry and frustrated by incompetence.

The guide was very nice and truly apologetic for our wait. "First you must see a video of the construction of the dam. It is in English. The others saw the Spanish version, and have already left by bus to see the dam."

"But, I want to see the dam," I said impatiently, not wanting to waste time looking at a boring video.

"Don't worry. I'll take you to the dam with my pickup, and we'll catch up to the tour. But first you must see the video."

Obviously, the routine of the tour could not be altered, and I resigned myself, as Doris keeps telling me to "go with the flow."

The video was very well done with English sub-titles, and I enjoyed the tale of the giant dam's construction and engineering. Afterward we waited. And waited. Just the two of us in a very quiet, empty room.

"You liked the video, didn't you?" asked Doris.

"Yeah. What about you?" I asked.

"It was okay as dams go, but not as much fun as a good mystery or love story."

"Right," I said, realizing we had a basic incompatibility where dams were concerned.

"Come on," she said, "let's go down and see the receptionist again. Maybe she can find our guide, but I bet we'll never catch up to the tour."

We found our guide, and she got us into her shiny white pickup assuring us that we would catch up to the tour. She tore along a narrow road contouring a moderately steep hillside, no tour bus in sight.

Where's the dam?

Then I realized this boring grassy hillside was the dam when I saw the top silhouetted in a straight knife edge against the murky white sky. At well over four and a half miles it was too long for me to see both ends at once. Good grief, there could have been a dozen buses lost out there without my seeing any one of them.

We caught up to our tour just as they were leaving the powerhouse.

"Go in for a quick look," said our guide. "We'll catch them at the next stop."

"A powerhouse," said Doris scrambling out of the pickup, "just what I've always wanted to see."

We stood on a viewing balcony at one end of a vast room. The far wall was lost in the distance, over a half-mile away. The noise was like thunder that never ended, and I felt uneasy on the vibrating, shaking balcony.

This is worse than an earthquake, it never ends.

"Let's go," said Doris. "All we can see are those little

round metal things down on the floor all in a row and all alike."

"Whoa," I said. "Each of those little round things are over fifty feet in diameter, much bigger than our house. Did you count how many there were?"

"I tried, but I lost track at twelve."

"I can't count them all either, but I read in a brochure that they have eighteen of them, and all together they produce more electricity than ten nuclear power plants."

As we left, I thought, *This isn't the largest dam or the largest reservoir; it's only the largest producer of power in the world. That sounds great, but there's not much to see. Boring* came to mind.

We found our tour group stopped at a viewpoint and our guide let us off to join them, before she dashed off in her shiny white pickup. Everyone was out looking around, so we looked around too. The grassy slope of the dam extended on ahead for what seemed like miles. It was split just in front of the viewpoint by a concrete spillway, completely dry. All the water from the Rio Parana flowed through the turbines, and we saw where the water from them welled up quietly to form a river again below the dam. This was the last stop on the tour, and on the way back to the visitor center, Doris and I remained silent for awhile.

"This was not a very exciting tour. Not much to see," I finally said.

"I'm glad you said that, because I didn't think much of it either."

"Yeah," I said, "and we had to endure this heat and

everything else for practically nothing. This is not turning out to be a very good day."

But, worse was to come.

On the way back to the hole in the fence our friendly guards waved to us as we went by the gate they were guarding. Back at the bus stop a man was sitting in the shade of a tree in a lawn chair, and I figured he was waiting for a bus too. We talked a little and he introduced us to his little boy playing around in the dirt, throwing things, and doing small boy things. Then he told us he was a taxi driver. That put a crimp in the conversation, but Doris, ever polite if not extremely talkative to taxi drivers, continued with small talk about his son, the weather, anything but taxis.

"Yes, I drive taxi," he said proudly, ignoring Doris' comments about his boy.

"Is the weather always this warm?' asked Doris

"My big son brings taxi to me here, and then I drive to the city."

"Do you have any more children?" asked Doris.

"The bus will not come for a long time," he responded.

"How long?" I asked.

"I don't know," he said with a big grin and a shrug. "Many times they late. Very late."

"Don't you dare ask about a ride," said Doris to me in a low voice.

But, the words were out of my mouth before I could stop them. I'm sure it was the devil that made me ask.

"How much to take us to the bus terminal in the city?"

"*Diez mil,*" he said without hesitation. "Ten thousand guarani,"

"That's about five dollars," I said to Doris. "Maybe we should take him up on his offer. No telling how long we may have to wait here and the price is very good."

"No way," she said. "What taxi driver sits around in a lawn chair waiting for his taxi to arrive? Besides, he has shifty eyes."

"Oh come on. At this point you think all cab drivers have shifty eyes."

"How can you forget the last greedy driver we had just a couple hours ago who tried to cheat us."

"Don't worry, I'll make sure we all understand the price, and besides we can always call for a policeman."

A few minutes later, the taxi, an unmarked car drove up, and after the driver parked, he waved toward the man seated with us, and walked off without a word. The taxi driver stood up, folded his chair, and spoke to his boy.

"Are you going to the city now?" I asked.

"Si," he said. "I take you to bus terminal."

"Are you sure the price is ten mil."

"Of course," he said in exasperation. "I tell you before, ten mil"

"Doris, we've been here for quite awhile and no bus. Also, I don't see any other potential riders waiting. That should tell us something about its probability to arrive any time soon."

"Okay," she said reluctantly, "but I don't want any trouble with this man when we get there."

Before we got into the car, I wrote ten thousand

guarani on a piece of paper, and showed it to the driver. He nodded vigorously muttering "*Si, si.*"

Everything went well until he turned off the main road insisting we visit a natural history museum.

"We don't want a tour," I exclaimed. And then in a louder voice, "Just take us to the bus station."

"Please be my guests," he said. "No cost. I show you and my son this beautiful museum."

The best I could do was getting him to agree to limit our time for the visit to forty-five minutes. True to his word it didn't cost us a dime and he was a good guide, cheerfully escorting us among his favorite exhibits. The cool air inside the museum provided welcome relief from the grinding heat outside. At his urging we took several pictures, most of which included his son in different poses. Cute, but pesky. By this time the boy was talking to Doris and they seemed to be having a great time, even though Doris doesn't like museums.

I fumed and fidgeted as my mandated time ran out. We approached one hour as I stood looking at stuffed birds lined up in endless rows. Angry at last, I dragged Doris toward the entry, and told the driver we were leaving. The heat outside hit me like a physical blow, and I staggered for a step or two. A thermometer on the wall outside registered forty nine degrees centigrade which I figured was awfully close to 120 degrees Fahrenheit.

"How can we leave without our driver?" she sputtered. "We still have to get to the bus station."

"We'll hitchhike if we have to," I said in a low voice through gritted teeth.

"Okay, okay, but calm down," she said.

The driver caught up to us in the parking lot, and graciously, with a big grin, ushered us into his pseudo-taxi. A short time later we arrived at the bus terminal, all of us chattering away like old friends. But when I tendered the fare with a ten-mill note, and got ready to leave his taxi, the driver got very quiet. He refused to take the money, and his grin turned into a scowl.

Uh oh. Please, not another taxi driver incident.

"Diez dolares," he said.

"Ten dollars?" I asked. "But you agreed to take us for ten thousand guarani. See it's written on this paper, and you agreed to that amount. At least three times."

"I knew it," Doris muttered in the background.

I tried to give the ten-mill note to the driver again, but he pushed my arm away with a brusque gesture while practically shaking his head off his shoulders. He spoke in loud, rapid-fire Spanish, but the only thing I understood was *diez dolares* which came through loud and clear several times.

"Don't give the bastard a single dime more than he deserves," said Doris, entering the fray with her fiery temper beginning to show.

"We'll talk to a policeman at the terminal," I said.

With that, we got out of the taxi, and headed for the bus station. The driver and his son followed with the driver hurling what sounded like epitaphs at our backs. In one corner of the station we found a uniformed security guard in a little cubbyhole of an office. He listened to the driver spouting rapid Spanish, but drew a blank when we tried to explain our side, using baby Spanish mixed with English. I think Doris threw a little French into the mix. The driver figured that yelling and interrupting us would further his cause and he became progressively louder and more obnoxious. Finally, the guard threw his hands in the air and gave up. He sent an aide out for help and the little room got very quiet. The driver fidgeted with his hat, looking everywhere except at us. The little boy held on to his father's trousers, and looked up at us with big round eyes.

"The guard is probably getting an interpreter," I whispered to Doris.

Wrong. In a few minutes a real policeman came in looking more like the State military police. He had all the police accessories from helmet to leather jacket to jack boots, and I was reminded of men in armor. He had a big pistol at his side with cartridges in a belt around his waist. He carried a big stick and a mean-looking scowl. His side kick stood by the door with an automatic weapon at the ready.

Interpreters? Wrong. This was the Gestapo.

He spoke first to the driver who replied in fluent Spanish. Then he turned to me, ignoring Doris. Obviously she didn't count for much in his world. I started to explain what had happened, but he cut me off in mid-sentence. He probably couldn't figure out what I was saying, and didn't want to take the time to try. Or, maybe he liked taxi drivers.

"Pay," said the Gestapo man in English. He said a lot of other things too, but I couldn't understand all of them. I decided not to ask him to repeat or slow down his speech.

"But," I sputtered, "See, look," and I showed him the paper with ten thousand guarani written on it.

He glanced at it, brushed it aside, and in a snarling voice said, "Pay!"

Maybe that's all the English he knows.

Then Doris weighed in. "He's a lying no-good bastard. He cheats. Throw him in jail. He's not even a taxi driver. And if I get close enough to him, I'll kick him in the balls so hard he won't walk for a week!"

She said a lot of other unladylike things until the policeman turned to me, and said, "Keep your *esposa* under control, or I will deport both of you out of the country."

With that he pulled handcuffs off his multi-purpose belt.

Wow, I understood that pretty easily, but how do I control an angry, rampaging Doris, for crying-out-loud.

"Knock it off," I said, turning to Doris. " This guy is going to deport us if you keep on yelling. Look he's already got the handcuffs out, ready to use."

"Well, let him," she said, with only a little less volume.

"Do you really want to create an international incident over a lousy extra five dollars?"

"Sure, I would. If I'm right, I don't care."

Headlines in newspapers around the world came to mind screaming how two older, ugly Americans were deported from Paraguay for non-payment of their cab fare.

But she did quiet down, and the policeman turned

back to the driver who was complaining about the pictures we took at the museum with his son in them. He knew the cab fare decision was in his favor and tried to push the envelope to get a little more money out of us for those pictures. Doris cursed him again, tearing the film out of her camera. Exposing the entire roll, she threw the film at the driver.

"There, take your dumb pictures, and see how much good they'll do you."

Oh Lordy, we're going to be thrown out of Paraguay after all.

But the driver and the policeman remained curiously silent. I don't think they had ever seen anything quite like Doris before.

Into that vacuum I said to the driver, "Here's your money, but I have to subtract out the cost of the film we just gave you, so the total is seven dollars."

The driver started to protest, but the policeman cut him off with a few curt words. Then the driver took his son by the hand and walked away without another word. I thought we had won the policeman's heart until he turned back to us with a grim look on his face.

"Get out of this city," he said, "before nightfall."

Just like the movies where the sheriff tells the bad guys to leave town or else. That wouldn't be a hardship for us. We already had bus tickets and a great desire to leave his city anyway.

Later, waiting for our bus out of town, I said, "Doris, we've got to change our attitudes. How many seventy-two-year-old people do you know that have come close to being deported and then run out of town on the same day?"

"I don't know of any," she said with a grin, "but I thought it was kind of fun. And did you see that cab driver's face when I threw the film at him?" she said gleefully.

"No, I was waiting for the policeman to shoot us."

Holy Wells of Ireland

Points of interest on our maps of Ireland were marked in red to the extent that Ireland appeared to have a rash or a bad case of measles. Hundreds of these notations were for holy wells strewn throughout the country.

Doris and I did a lot of our traveling in the countryside of Ireland on rented bicycles, pedaling off the beaten track where few cars tended to go. . We got to see many holy wells because they provided a good excuse for us to stop pedaling and rest. Actually, I needed the rest more than Doris, who at seventy was older than I but in better shape. She thought that gave her some bragging rights, but I didn't think so.

I heard about holy wells before I left to visit Ireland. I couldn't figure out why so many wells were holy. Was there an act of a miracle to make it holy? Or, were all wells in Ireland just naturally holy to start with? To add to my confusion, when I got there I found that holy wells were actually holy springs. Like magic, water flowed out naturally from rock outcroppings or hillsides.

Celtic ancestors dammed the water into pools adjacent to the source before allowing it to runoff. The pools were deep enough for people to fill their buckets easily. Over the years others built steps down for easy access to the pool, and eventually enclosed the pool with protective walls and roof. Many of these little springhouses were quite elaborate with windows and doorways and cupola shaped roofs.

People propitiated the gods of the well with offerings of coins, special stones, or little plastic toys. The latter have grown to fairly large piles, but the coins never appeared to be overly dense, perhaps as a result of discreet harvesting.

Before we left for Ireland good friends told us to respect the sanctity of holy wells. They had tried to find the one true St. Patrick's well, but discovered many wells purporting to be St. Patrick's well, and in frustration, had blasphemed one or two of them in passing. St. Patrick must have heard, because they immediately became violently ill. It lasted until they made appropriate amends at the next available holy well. They didn't mean to imply they believed in a holy well power, but felt that under the circumstances it might be wise for us to be a little cautious around those wells.

Doris took their advice, and offered a special stone at each well we visited, adding it to the neat little pile of stones already there. We made sure to speak reverently at each site. All went well until we visited the holy well of St. Bridget. This saint was very special to Doris, because St. Bridget's love for children and animals reminded her of her deceased son who had similar feelings in his lifetime.

A busload of people was in the little grotto enclosing

the pool of water making it difficult for us to get near. They were in the process of leaving, but some were slow, and Doris was impatient. Taking up even more time, a few awkwardly reached into the pool with their Coke bottles to get some holy water to take home with them.

Doris muttered some picturesque and inappropriate words about these people in the way, and St. Bridget must have heard them. Doris didn't get sick, nor did anything bad happen to her physically. But, one week later when we were home, Doris's car was in a terrible wreck. At a stoplight the truck in front of us didn't go when the light turned green, but she did. As a result, Doris had eight thousand dollars worth of damage to the front end of her car. The truck had none, and worse, she got the ticket.

To my credit, I didn't mention her relapse at the St. Bridget holy well, nor am I sure those events are even connected. And I certainly don't subscribe to supernatural powers, but I would advise anyone to be a little careful around those holy wells of Ireland.

Romanian Hospitality

We boarded the train for Bacau at noon just before it left the station, and hurriedly looked for seats. The first few compartments were too full of people and bundles, and we kept on looking, staggering down the aisle of the swaying coach. In another compartment, a young man sat leaning forward on his seat talking earnestly to a pretty young woman in the seat across from him. They spoke in Romanian and his words were partially drowned by the clackity-clack of the wheels on rails. They appeared oblivious to our presence.

"Let's find another place to sit," said Doris in a low voice. "I don't want to intrude."

"That's okay with me," I said, starting to back out of the compartment.

The girl looked up at us and began to speak before we had a chance to leave. "Where you from?" she asked in accented English.

"We're from the United States," said Doris, smiling at her.

"Oh please, stay. Sit with us," she said in a delightful accent, smiling back at Doris. "We would love to talk to you and practice English, wouldn't we Mario?"

Mario sitting across from her didn't look too enthusiastic, and I got the impression that we were indeed interrupting his plans for the afternoon.

"I'm Anka, and this is Mario," she said pointing to the young man who still hadn't said a word. *Maybe he doesn't know any English.* Anka's face was open and alive with expression, whereas Mario's face remained deadpan, almost sullen. He was thin and wiry, but Anka was the picture of a healthy, expansive young woman in action.

To make room for us, Anka had already moved herself and her things across the aisle to sit next to Mario. I'm sure that brightened up his day a little.

"We travel all morning from Bucharest," said Anka. "In Bacau, we get off train."

"We started out this morning, too," said Doris, "from that what-do-you-call-it town?"

Then she looked to me for help, because she rarely knew the names of places.

"We came over from Brasov to catch this train," I said, not mentioning to Doris that it was only the second largest city in Romania.

"I knew it was something like that," said Doris.

"Where are you going?" asked Mario. *Wow. He speaks good English.*

"We stop for the night at Radouti," I said, "From there we'll visit some of the old wooden monasteries with painted murals on their walls."

"Very nice," said Mario, nodding with a hint of a smile.

With that, the four of us started a conversation that

lasted all afternoon. The women talked the most, naturally. I did fairly well, breaking into their chattering now and then, but Mario stayed pretty quiet, pensive perhaps. Time flew by and the train seemed to go faster, too. Anka worked as a nanny in Germany, and Mario worked on cruise ships in the Caribbean and Alaska. Both were on the way to visit their parents in Bacau. They grew up in Bacau and went to high school together.

"Looks like both of you went a long way from home to find work," I said.

"There is no work here in Romania," said Mario, shrugging and spreading his hands palms up. "Everyone leaves."

"I thought I had a teaching job in Bucharest," said Anka, with a just a touch of a frown on her face, "but the person I was supposed to replace changed her mind and didn't quit, so I went to Germany to work."

"We used to go out on dates," said Mario. "But that was a long time ago, and we have not seen each other since leaving Bacau.

"Yes," said Anka, glancing at Mario sideways with a cute smile. "I was surprised to see Mario on the same train with me."

They were obviously happy to see each other again, and it seemed from the glances and furtive touches that the romance was taking up where it had left off.

Later, Doris told me, "Anka was happy we came along when we did to sit in their coach. She really didn't want to be alone with Mario."

"Why is that?" I asked. "She sure seemed to be enjoying his attention."

"She felt uncomfortable and thought the romancing with Mario was proceeding too fast, and she wanted to slow things down a little." *Doris and I, chaperones? How do women learn to be so devious?*

About ten minutes before the train was due to arrive in Bacau, Mario broke into the conversation and stopped it cold with his longest dialogue of the day. "Stay tonight in Bacau," he said sternly, "and catch the train to Radouti tomorrow. Get off the train with us. You can stay at my parent's apartment and sleep in my old bedroom. Tomorrow we'll go sightseeing."

All was quiet a few seconds to allow that novel idea to sink in.

Finally, I turned to Doris and said, "We've got to get to Radouti sometime, but it's not far from Bacau. We can get off here if you want, and get another train tomorrow. We'd lose a little money in train fare, but that's not very much."

"It's okay with me," said Doris. "But Mario, will it be okay with your parents if we come to their home? After all, they're not here to make this decision."

"Of course, it's no problem," he said, with a wave of his hand.

Well, if it is, we can always get a hotel, I thought.

Until then, Anka had been silent. Now, she enthusiastically agreed to the plan.

"Then it's settled," said Mario, and he broke into one of his rare smiles.

"I'll agree to get off with you," I said, "under one condition."

That got their complete attention and everyone looked at me.

"Alright," said Doris, impatiently. "What?"

"Mario and Anka have to agree to allow us to take them out to dinner. It has to be a typical Romanian meal in a nice restaurant."

"What a good idea," said Doris.

"Oh, we'd love to," said Anka, "but are you sure you want to do that?"

"Absolutely," said Doris, thereby sealing the deal.

Mario didn't say anything, but had a big grin on his face like the cat that ate the canary.

Was he somehow controlling all this? I bet Anka is one of the sights he plans to see tomorrow.

We shared a taxi from the train station and dropped Anka off at her home on the way to Mario's parents' flat. Doris and I had a little time to freshen up—rinse our faces that is. Meanwhile, Mario changed into some tight-fitting slacks and a t-shirt with a deep V neckline, showing off a gold chain entwined with some tufts of chest hair. By now I was hoping Anka would dump the guy.

Mario wrote a short note about us to his parents who weren't home from work yet. Anka showed up driving her family car under strict parental instructions that she was the only one to be driving it. She was dressed in a miniskirt that barely covered the parts that needed covering. She wore tight-fitting, calf-length boots with high heels, and a long-sleeved white blouse open enough in the front to show off the tops of very pretty, white, robust breasts. Although I enjoyed the show, I'm sure she hadn't dressed that way for me.

Doris told me later that Anka felt safe to "dress up" since we would be with them throughout the evening." *Chaperoning again?*

"I didn't know she planned to wear something so provocative. She was dressed fit to kill," Doris said.

I thought the restaurant was a disappointment. The food was far more cosmopolitan than Romanian. They didn't even have pork or cabbage on the menu. However, the entry to the restaurant was fun with lush exotic plants and trees growing inside a glass enclosure. A small rivulet burbled between little pools set in natural rock grottos. But the main attraction was a six-foot high thin curtain of water that fell noisily into one of the larger grottos with green ferns and other water-loving plants growing among the glistening water-soaked rocks.

After dinner, Anka drove us to a roadhouse about forty minutes out of the city.

"What's a roadhouse?" asked Doris, snuggling against me in the dark back seat. *Good grief, are we going to need chaperones too?*

It's like a country club," said Mario, "Where people go to drink beer and dance until all hours of the night. They usually have live music."

"I don't know, this is a Tuesday tonight," said Anka. "My mother used to work out there part-time and she said Mondays and Tuesdays were pretty quiet."

Anka was an aggressive driver, taking curves at full

speed, and screaming down the straight-aways as if at the Indianapolis speedway. Doris quickly lost interest in me and sat bolt upright, clutching my arm and an armrest to keep an even keel. I found it soothing to keep my eyes closed and think of other things.

The roadhouse reminded me of a typical grange hall, a square no-nonsense building with one big room. A bar extended across one end of the room with a postage-stamp-sized dance floor and a bandstand set in front of it. At the opposite end were the toilet rooms. The bulk of the room was taken up by trench tables in long rows and benches, reminding me of the Oktoberfest tents in Munich. I half expected to see buxom young ladies running around in their tight-fitting dirndls with foaming tankards of beer in hand. As predicted, the roadhouse was quiet.

"We are early," said Anka, plopping down at one of the empty tables. "It might get a little more active later, but I don't think so. Not tonight."

A few other couples sat strewn about the room quietly talking. The big noise came from a loud, bulky stereo playing strident American rock music. *Can't get away from that stuff even in Eastern Europe.* We ordered Cokes in deference to Anka who couldn't drink anything with alcohol, because she was the one driving that night. *MADD mothers had gotten to Romania.*

"Sometimes this place is so packed with people and noise, I can't talk or think," said Anka looking around at the nearly empty room and shaking her head slightly.

"Is that fun?" I asked.

"Of course," said Anka, jumping up and grabbing Mario's arm to drag him out to the dance floor.

After the second round of Coke we all were ready to go. A few more people had drifted in, but even I could guess that the roadhouse would not rock this evening. Anka must have broken the all-time speed record driving us back to Bacau. I told Doris later that she had only two gears: fast and stop. She dropped us off at Mario's flat before careening off to her home. *Such a pretty girl, but what a menace on the road.*

As we watched her speed away, Mario informed us, "Anka will join us tomorrow to go sightseeing, but my father will be driving." *How does he set all this stuff up so fast?*

We met Mario's parents, Speranta and Nicolae, who were waiting for us with a complete home-cooked dinner. I groaned inwardly at the thought of eating more food so late at night. But how could we refuse?

Doris whispered to me, "I can't eat all this. I'll be sick."

"You'll have to try," I said. "Just eat real slowly whatever you can."

We sat in their kitchen, and ate roasted paprika chicken, shredded cabbage with a slightly sour tangy taste, stuffed green peppers, and cut-up cucumbers in yogurt. And Romanian beer. With Mario's help as translator, we talked nonstop with Speranta and Nicolae throughout the meal, and they became good friends.

Then Nicolae got up and brought out a bottle of slivovitz, a strong plum brandy, and we began drinking toasts to country, God, motherhood, each other, and anything else we could think of. I think Doris took one sip and gave it up, leaving more for the rest of us. Soon after, Mario went to bed, but we didn't need him anymore to translate. Doris and Speranta washed the dishes and cleaned up the kitchen while chatting and laughing as women do everywhere. Against that background of pleasant sounds, Nicolae and I worked very hard, and finally managed to kill off that bottle of slivovitz with our endless toasts.

The next morning we jumped into Nicolae's car and, true to Mario's prediction, went over to pick up Anka who joined us for the day. We never saw Speranta again; she had already gone to work and would be there long after we left Bacau. Anka came running out and squeezed into the front seat between Mario and his dad, as Anka's parents waved to us from the balcony of their second-floor flat. She and Mario now wore casually conservative, conventional clothes. Loose-fitting, too. *That part of the show was over.*

We drove about fifty miles out into the country where Nicolae was building a small store/cafe on a busy main highway to serve food and drink to the traveling public. It was too far away to serve as a typical roadhouse for party goers from Bacau. He had a dream to be self-employed in his own business, and live out there in the country.

The property was about one hundred feet wide by perhaps five hundred feet deep to a river bordering on the back. He grew vegetables, fruit trees, and flowers. Chickens roamed at will, and two friendly dogs guarded the property. After a tour of the work site and grounds, we sat together at a table under a shade tree, set with a platter piled high with sliced watermelon. Nicolae served us peach liquor and we talked and laughed, ate pieces of ripe sweet melon, and sipped our drinks. Nicolae spent a lot of time off to one side fussing with some meat on a wood-fired grille. Suddenly, Anka and Mario disappeared. I didn't even see them go. *So much for my chaperoning abilities.*

"What now?" I asked. "Is Mario about to make his move?"

"Don't worry about it," said Doris. "Anka doesn't like him all that well."

"How do you know that?"

"Because she told me."

"I didn't hear anything like that."

"You men never do really hear women when we talk. You, especially."

Oops, I had heard that one before. Fortunately, Nicolae came back from massaging the meat, and I didn't have to respond. The errant couple returned in time to enjoy lunch: grilled pork, cabbage slaw, and cut-up tomatoes and onions mixed with generous slabs of feta cheese. After lunch the plum brandy made its magical appearance again, but I insisted on only one shot, and by extension only one toast.

Time passed quickly with easy conversation and laughter, and the hour of catching the train to Radouti arrived quickly, too.

"We must get back to the train station," I said, "and continue our travels."

Mario, Anka, and Nicholai pleaded with us.

"Don't go," said Anka. "Stay one more night."

"Take the train tomorrow, but stay with us one more night," said Mario.

"We need to go," I said. "We've lost one day already and we can't afford to lose more time." *What am I doing? It doesn't really matter that much whether we stay or go.*

"Please stay," said Nicholai. "Speranta will join us and we'll have a big barbeque feast this evening, with lots of wine. We'll sit around a fire and sing, and camp out for the night. And take you to the train station tomorrow."

"I'm sorry," I said. "We really would like to stay, but we can't afford to lose another day from our itinerary." *Good grief. I'm the one who always says itineraries are made to be broken. What a hypocrite.*

Mario, with Anka along for company, drove us to the station, and they waited with us on the platform for the train to arrive. Mario introduced us to a young woman he knew that was going on the same train to Radouti, and asked her to look after us. The train arrived, and we said final goodbyes. Doris had tears in her eyes as we waved to them when the train pulled out of the station. To her credit, Doris never questioned me about my decision to leave Bacau in the face of such genuine requests to stay. After all, I was in charge of our precious itinerary.

I knew we made choices every day that affected the direction of our travels, who we met and what we experienced. We had already changed our destiny the day before by getting off the train in Bacau instead of going on to Radouti. And now, another door was to open, because we were on the train to Radouti, today, not tomorrow.

Nicholai, Mario, Anka, and I enjoy watermelon and peach wine.

More Romanian Hospitality

About halfway to Radouti our train stopped at a small station in the middle of nowhere, and all the people in our coach left.

"Why is everyone leaving?" I asked, looking around at the empty car.

"I don't know," said Doris. "Maybe we should leave, too."

"But why? And where in the heck are we?"

In a minute or two the little platform outside our window was empty, and I had a queasy feeling in the pit of my stomach. Something was wrong.

"Let's get off the train," I said, standing up to pull my pack off the overhead rack.

"What?" said Doris. "Are you sure?"

"No, but we just can't sit here not knowing what's going on."

Suddenly, a young woman burst into the compartment. She was agitated and out of breath when she came running up to us.

"Come," she said. "You must get out. Now, please."

Doris and I didn't say a word as we hoisted our packs to our backs and prepared to abandon the train. We followed her down the aisle to the end of the coach but, instead of getting off, she led us into the next coach and on into the one beyond. I didn't count the empty coaches, but we finally arrived in a coach full of people, and she ushered us into a compartment where two others were seated.

"I'm Donna," she said, as she invited us to sit. "This train is small now, and your coach where you sat does not go to Radouti. Everyone must get off here and change to coaches going all the way."

"I remember you now," said Doris. "You're Mario's friend, the one he introduced us to back at Bacau, while we were waiting for this train."

"Yes," said Donna. "He tell me to take care of you."

Just then we felt the train jerk, and start to move forward. I looked out the window and, sure enough, the back half of the train including our original coach remained motionless. I watched as we left it behind. *She sure did look after us.*

"Thank you for your help," I said. "We could have been left behind, stuck out in the boondocks."

She smiled with a puzzled look on her face. "What is that?"

"He means left behind in the countryside," said Doris, looking at me with a slight frown.

Doris and I try not to use idioms, slang, or unusual words when traveling in foreign countries, because many people just don't understand what we're saying.

Donna smiled and shrugged, "It was nothing." Then

turning to the other people in the compartment, she said. "This is my sister, Anna, and my grandfather."

Granddad said nothing and barely glanced at us before turning back to stare out his window. But Anna jumped up with a smile and gave Doris a little hug as she said, "I'm so glad to see you. I'm sixteen and learn English in school so I can get a good job when I'm older. Where do you come from?"

"We're from United States," said Doris.

"Americans," she said in astonishment. Then she said a word in Romanian that I easily translated to, "Wow."

Turning to Donna, Doris asked, "Are you in school, too?"

"No, I'm twenty-one, and work in an office. I'm a clerk. We were visiting my aunt in Bacau, and now we go to our home in Radouti."

Soon the three; Doris, Donna, and Anna were talking gaily among themselves while granddad and I watched the world go silently by our windows. *How do I tell which is Donna or Anna?* I mused. *Well, Donna, the older one, is dark haired with a curlier hairstyle and Anna has straight, light-brown hair. Also, Anna, the younger, is more talkative and laughs easier. She also speaks better English.*

When the train arrived in Radouti we said goodbye to the girls, and they left with Granddad following close behind. We were slow getting off the train and paused on the platform to get our bearings to determine which direction to look for a hotel. That was a problem whenever we arrived in a strange place, orienting ourselves on the little, small-scale maps furnished in the guidebook. So, with my eyes on the map, I didn't see Donna running across the platform toward us. Suddenly, there she was in front of us, out of breath again.

"Come home with us," she said. "Don't go to a hotel."

"Oh that's very sweet of you," said Doris, "but don't worry about us. We're used to finding a place to stay."

I caught sight of Anna and the grandfather waiting at the edge of the platform.

"You don't need to find a place," said Donna. "Please come with us. We want you to stay at our house tonight."

"It's your call, Doris," I said.

"But your parents won't be expecting us," said Doris.

"It's okay," said Donna. "Please come."

Then Donna took Doris' hand and led her, with me following, across the platform to where the others waited. Anna was practically jumping up and down with excitement as she took Doris' other hand, and we all started walking down the street away from the station. With Donna and Anna on each side of her talking away, I followed their rapid pace as best I could. Even so, I was out of breath within four blocks, and had to stop a few seconds. Granddad stalked on ahead and soon disappeared. We never did see him again.

The sisters' home was way out on the edge of town, quite a distance from the train station. We walked up the driveway to the back of the house and came face to face with Mom and Dad. Donna explained we were staying the night and their mouths dropped open a little and their eyes widened as they stared at us. A puzzled look came to Mom's face, probably thinking of where to put these strangers and what to feed them.

I said, "Donna look, if this is too hard for your parents, we can simply get a hotel in town. We don't want to be an imposition."

Almost in desperation, she said, "It's okay, it's okay. Please, it's okay."

Then she grabbed my arm and pulled me closer to her family. Dad was first to recover from the shock.

He smiled and shook hands saying, "Dutu," pointing to himself and repeating, "Dutu."

Donna introduced her mother, Nuta. Nuta had recovered a little from her surprise, and invited us into her house to remove our packs. She had a round face with the edges of her mouth turned down to make her look permanently unhappy. The back door seemed to be the major entrance to the house, and shoes lined the outside step. We left our shoes at the doorway and entered an enclosed porch. Donna and her mother talked rapidly in Romanian before they invited us into the next room.

"This is my bedroom," said Donna, "and you sleep here tonight. I sleep with Anna."

While dropping our packs, Nuta stripped the bed and shook the pillows out of their slips, preparing to change the bedding for us. She had a grim look on her unsmiling face, wasting no time getting things into proper order. Donna gathered some personal stuff that she needed for the night, and took them to Anna's room in the attic. She reached that room by climbing a ladder in the entryway near the door. Anna had disappeared, and Doris and I tried to stay out of the way of a rampaging Nuta on a mission.

A partition cut across the enclosed porch separating the entry part from Donna's bedroom. A huge ceramic wood stove dominated her small room leaving barely enough space for a bed, dresser, and a pathway to the bed. I figured the stove probably heated the whole house and, when in use, would make Donna's bedroom intolerably hot.

An older woman, about our age, bustled in with Anna. Donna came rushing down the ladder to greet her, and introduced us to a beaming Marie, the grandmother. Marie insisted that we go to her house next door, and as we and the girls left, Nuta was hauling blankets out of storage. She still hadn't said a word to us since our introductions. Nuta didn't speak any English, and let us know it.

Marie was delighted to have us at her house. She presented Doris with a flower, and then rummaged about to find a lace doily she had made, and gave that to Doris, too. Then, she gave Doris a big hug with a kiss on each cheek. We felt very welcome, although Granddad remained out of sight and out of sound. *Out of mind, too.*

We sat at the kitchen table with Donna and Anna, while Marie served watermelon, all the while talking and smiling, and fussing over all of us. It was obvious she had a special relationship with her grandchildren. Doris figured she probably took care of those girls all their lives while both parents worked.

When we returned to our "home," Nuta was busy in

the kitchen where Marie joined her shortly. We followed Donna into the backyard where Dutu sat on a small stool in front of a makeshift grill, tending a fire, using corncobs for fuel. Donna and Anna showed us the outhouse and the shower before it got too dark to see.

The outhouse sat next to the chicken coop inside the chicken pen. To get to it, we went through a gate in a fence that kept chickens separated in their own part of the backyard. Clucking and squawking chickens dashed willy-nilly out of our way as we followed a dirt walkway covered with their slippery slimy droppings right up to the entrance of the outhouse. We tried sidestepping the mess but too much of it littered the entire area inside the fence. And the smell in the yard was far worse than in the outhouse. With no way to dodge the droppings, we resorted to plowing straight through the mess. Obviously, Nuta didn't want shoes dripping with chicken excrement in her house, so that's why everyone removed shoes at the door before entering.

An elevated tank with a showerhead attached stood prominently at the end of the walkway directly in front of the outhouse. By pulling on a rope, water was released through the showerhead and, presto, a cold-water shower. But the shower had no cover, no walls, no curtains, just the great outdoors. Any bather would be exposed to one and all as well as to the weather, while standing barefoot in an oozy, smelly mess. Although invited to take a shower we politely passed up the opportunity. I figured that in the winter that shower got very little use.

We returned to Dutu and sat on little stools watching

him roast sausages over coals that glowed red in the gathering dark. Relaxed and sipping a beer, I felt the fire's heat and smelled the smoke as the meat sizzled and spat grease into the fire. The girls stood close to Doris, watching her every move, and I heard the soft voices of the other women inside making supper.

Neighborhood men came to visit Dutu, and in the process look us over. They spoke only to him, and tried not to stare at us. Dutu was a jovial host engaging his visitors with talk and laughter. When they left they would acknowledge us with a nod of the head and a Romanian "good night." Word got around fast that Dutu was entertaining Americans, people from another world, and for a brief time he was famous. When the sausages were done we all left to go inside. The night had turned chilly, and I was glad to leave Dutu's dying coals to sit at a table in Nuta's warm, oversized kitchen.

Odors of cooking cabbage filled the air, almost drowning out the slight smell of wood smoke. A jet black, wood-burning cook stove and oven squatted against one wall. On one side of it a refrigerator purred, and on the other a sink with drain boards attached stood on four legs. A hose through the wall provided fresh running water, controlled through a hose bibb valve.

The resulting wastewater made disgusting noises as it gargled and sucked its way out through a pipe in the wall below the sink. From there the wastewater drained across the back yard in an open ditch into the chicken pen. The system provided primitive indoor plumbing and a laborsaving way to water the chickens. Not bad, except for those sucking sounds, that only quit when the water stopped flowing.

Cupboards reaching to the ceiling were mounted above a large work counter which extended across another wall. Pots and pans, blackened on their bottoms, hung by their handles near the stove. Cold weather coats hung on pegs near the door to the entry porch. And someone, probably Dutu, had stockpiled a large amount of firewood near the stove. The only other room consisted of a sitting area/bedroom with a TV. A wide double doorway led directly into it from the kitchen. Basically, the four of them lived in a two-room house with a built-in porch and an attic.

Supper started out with a bowl of delicious spicy soup of indeterminate flavor. It was ladled from a huge black kettle that looked like a permanent part of the stove. I suspected the pot was bottomless; never empty, with fresh meat and veggies thrown in from time to time, along with leftovers to keep it ever ready to dispense soup any time of day or night. We ate sausages and potatoes, cabbage and bread, and a delicious salsa of chopped garlic and cream. Dutu served us his homemade wine, and dessert was rice that had been cooked in cream. Delicious.

All conversation flowed through Donna or Anna, who were pleased and excited by their important role as translators. Marie was the sparkplug of the family, laughing and talking, constantly jumping up to serve food and drink. Grandpa never showed up. We talked about what we had seen and done in Romania and what we liked. We talked about our children and home. Dutu joined in the fun with gestures and hearty laughter to make up for little English. But, Nuta was quiet and withdrawn, and rarely laughed.

At one point she made eye contact with me, and asked through our interpreters, "How much did it cost for you to come here?"

Startled, I tried to figure a way to answer without making her feel bad. I knew there existed a great difference between us, in costs and disposable income. I sidestepped the question a little by assuming that "here" meant anywhere in Europe.

"Five hundred dollars," I said, which was the cost for one of us to get to London. I didn't mention the additional costs to get from there to Romania.

They sat motionless, in complete silence, mentally computing this figure into lei, the Romanian currency, which we purchased at the rate of 7,200 to a dollar.

"But that's three-and-a-half million Lei," Donna said incredulously.

I nodded silently. *Yeah, seven million for two.*

"Oh, we can never do that," said Nuta. "It is impossible. I work with an accountant and make fifty dollars per month. Donna works as a secretary/clerk and makes thirty-five dollars per month."

She didn't say how much money Dutu made, but I estimated their total family income was probably close to one million lei per month. If their disposable income was anything like ours at home, they might be able to save ten percent, roughly one hundred thousand lei per month. Theoretically, they could, over a long period of time, save enough lei to make such a trip, but it would take a lot of desire and discipline.

"How much money do you make?" she asked, looking at me intently.

None of your business.

Uncomfortable at the way this conversation had turned, I sidestepped some more, and replied, "I'm in construction and don't get a monthly income. Only when the job is finished do I receive money, so my income varies greatly. I have to save up money a long time to come here."

The others at the table remained silent, listening intently as this uncomfortable conversation unfolded.

"It would take years," Nuta went on, "for us to make enough money to do a journey like yours. We will never be able to do that. People in your country must be very rich."

"That's not true. There are some people who are rich, but there are some people who are poor, and most of us are in between."

The silence in the room was deafening and went on for what seemed an eternity, as the family stared into space. Doris and I exchanged glances, and I saw her make a wry face and give a slight shrug.

Suddenly Dutu scraped his chair noisily back across the floor, startling all of us. He reached into a cupboard, and pulled out a bottle of plum brandy, the infamous slivovitz.

"Come on," he said, "let's have some toasts. Enough about money. It's evil, but this is good," and he poured out the first of many drinks.

It was good, and even Nuta mellowed a little. We went into the sitting room where Dutu played recordings of Romanian music. He sang along with the music now and then, and we joined the girls clapping in time with the music. Nuta listened and seemed content, and Grandma Marie cleaned up the kitchen. Finally, the music stopped, the liquor was gone, and Nuta, ever the "heavy" of the family, ended the fun by suggesting it was time for bed.

On the way to bed, I said to Doris, "Let's give Nuta some money to help her with the costs of our visit."

"I think that would be very nice," said Doris, "but I bet she won't accept our money."

Doris was right. Nuta forcefully shoved my hand with the money in it aside, and spoke some rapid Romanian to Donna to translate.

"She does not want payment," said Donna. "Please, you are guests. She says guests do not pay for hospitality at her house."

Sometime during the meal we had asked Donna if she would like to go with us on an overnight excursion to see some of the local monasteries, famous for their wooden churches with painted murals. We would pay for all of her costs. I don't know if she asked her mom, but her response was an enthusiastic yes.

Later when Doris and I were alone, I said, "I don't know why we didn't ask Anna to go with us, too. She's certainly old enough."

"She may have to be in school," said Doris, "and anyway, I don't think her mom would allow her to go off overnight with strangers."

Doris was wrong for a change. When we got up next morning Dutu and Nuta had already gone to work, but I asked Anna anyway, if she wanted to go. She became very excited and immediately called her mom at work. She got the okay to go with us which really surprised and pleased Doris. The four of us prepared for the journey with Grandma Marie fussing over her girls. They each carried a little daypack and had a few lei to spend for gifts.

Since we would not be coming back to Radaudi, Donna went to her dresser and brought out a six-inch-tall, non-descript ceramic vase and gave it to Doris, saying, "I give you this to remember us when you are back home."

This brought tears to Doris's eyes which wasn't unusual. She tended to cry over good things or bad, and many times I wasn't sure which it was. Marie gave us all hugs and sent us on our way. The older women cried a little, again, but the young women were far too excited to be concerned about a good-bye from their grandmother.

While the others were occupied with goodbyes and tears, I went to our bedroom and stuffed a pillowcase with some Romanian currency, one hundred thousand lei. That amounted to about fourteen dollars, which I knew could never cover the value of our experience with that family.

"I left them a gift, not a payment," I told Doris later. "Since we couldn't get to a store to buy them a gift before we got to their house, I had to leave money instead."

Doris's response was an enthusiastic hug and kiss. *Sometimes, I'm rewarded for getting things right.*

Dutu cooks sausages for supper.

A Romanian Excursion

We trusted our Romanian companions, Donna and Anna, to get us to the right place. After all, they spoke the language, and Donna had consulted the bus driver extensively. We were on our way to see the old monastery at Sucevita. The bus dropped us off in mid-afternoon, and then roared away leaving us on the edge of a lonely country road. Looking around me I saw farmland and a few scattered houses in a lush green landscape backed by small rolling hills leading to bigger and bigger hills with mountains in the distance.

Not much action here.

"Where's Sucevita?" I asked. "And which way is the monastery?"

"I do not know the village," said Donna. "I have never been here before, but the bus driver said the monastery is down this road," and she pointed in the direction we had been going while on the bus.

"It's okay," the younger sister, Anna, said to me with a reassuring grin. "This bus stop is the closest to the monastery. We will have to walk, maybe two kilometers."

I quickly figured that was a little over a mile. "Okay

we can walk there, but we'll have to find a place to stay the night."

"Let's just go to the monastery," said Doris. "Maybe we'll find a place on the way, or they'll tell us where to go when we get there."

With the girls leading, we walked at the edge of a lonely empty road. It reminded me of walking the empty streets of Putna for a mile or so that morning getting to the site of another monastery. *Not many cars in Romania.* At Putna, Donna and Anna alternately skipped ahead of us to investigate the way to the monastery, and then, ran back to see if we older folks needed help. Somewhat like puppies, free at last, to romp.

Walking through the village of Putna we passed small houses dominated by their oversized metal gutters. Each was somewhat different in design and a piece of artwork done in copper sheet metal, now turned from bright shiny copper to a dull greenish gray color. They provided a twelve to fifteen inch decorative border at the eaves, and depicted fruits and flowers, interspersed with intricate geometric designs embossed in the metal.

"I've never seen gutters like these before. Aren't they neat?" I asked.

"If you think so, yes," Doris replied with little enthusiasm.

"This place must have a master artisan to create such beautiful metal work," I went gushing on.

"Oh, look at those goats," said Doris. "Aren't they cute?"

I took picture after picture of decorated oversized

gutters and downspouts until Doris took the camera away from me. Then she took pictures of goats.

The Putna monastery, like many others we visited was surrounded by high, thick stone walls with towers at each corner. It looked more like a fort than a monastery. And like the others was designated a World Heritage site.

The church centered inside the walls, and built in the early 1500s, was the main focus of interest. It was a small, unimposing wooden building with a bell tower. Typically, the entry under the bell tower led directly into the nave. The area to the rear of the altar was enclosed by a semicircular wall. But its main feature was the massive overhanging eaves that projected out six to eight feet beyond the walls.

It was the murals painted on the walls of the church inside and outside that attracted visitors. The scenes shown were mostly biblical, although some depicted aspects of everyday life of that time. Because the oversized eaves protected the paintings outside, they retained their color and design like those on the inside, only a little diminished after five hundred years.

Doris and I could only look at so many pictures at a time before getting itchy to move on. The girls grew tired of them long before we did. They had already knelt before the altar and prayed a little, and were now investigating every square inch of the walled-in site. They made short forays away from where we stood, and returned regularly to check in, bubbling over with enthusiasm about the stuff we had to see. They chattered and laughed gesturing in the direction we needed to go before heading out again on their explorations.

We finally left Putna and took the bus to Sucevita where another old monastery was waiting for our visit. This was a larger, more famous site, but again the main focus for most visitors was the paintings on the walls of the church. We walked down the road toward it only a short distance before Donna spotted a house advertising rooms for rent.

"We can stay there tonight," she said, pointing across the road at the small house.

"Oh, let's," said Anna dashing across the road and into the front yard.

An older woman with a grim face stood waiting in the open doorway. I got the impression she waited there whenever the bus was scheduled to come by, at least until her rooms were rented. She showed us the two rooms she had, one up a steep stairway to the attic and one on the first floor. We took both rooms for eighty thousand lei, about eleven dollars, including breakfast. Both rooms were full of furniture which made it difficult to get to the bed, or move around. The heavy wooden furniture, ornately carved, gave the rooms an appearance of an antique shop, or a second-hand store. *Junk shop came to mind.* I thought maybe the owners had drastically downsized their dwelling space, but tried to keep all their heirlooms.

I picked the first floor room, because I wanted as few obstacles in the way as possible when I got up in the middle of the night to go to the outhouse. Doris and I dropped our packs and sat for a moment in peace and quiet. We heard the girls above us gaily talking while bustling about, settling in.

The outhouse was in the backyard, and a colorful collage of glossy pictures cut out of magazines covered the inside walls from floor to ceiling, and covered the ceiling too. The decorations helped to make a pause there more enlightening. The door was too short for me and I kept bumping my head on the top jamb. If I remembered to duck going in, I would forget going out, and got whacked again, much to my annoyance.

When I complained, Doris wasn't too sympathetic.

"We're only here for one night. Your head will survive even if you can't remember to duck."

That afternoon we walked up the road to visit the monastery. It was, like many of the others we visited, run by nuns. *Strange to find monasteries with no men around.* It seemed to me an oxymoron.

"How come nuns run a monastery?" I asked. "I can understand that there may not be enough monks around to operate the place, but why don't they hire men?"

"I'm not sure," said Doris, "but I know you men have a hard time keeping up a house, much less a big place like this."

The nuns enforced a strict dress code that prohibited men from showing their legs. Two young men showed up at the entrance wearing shorts and tried to get in, but those nuns were a tough bunch and cut them no slack. Their choices were to walk away or wear a wrap-around skirt provided by the nuns. They grinned sheepishly and wore their skirts with goodwill, if not with grace. Donna and Anna apparently got a kick out of watching men walk around in skirts. They pointed at them sauntering away and traded rapid bursts of Romanian punctuated by giggles.

We were finished with our visit when I said, "I'm hungry, let's get something to eat."

"We can eat right here," Anna replied, "the nuns will feed us. They feed everybody that's hungry. I've eaten in a monastery before."

"Well—I was thinking of a restaurant. Are you sure they will feed us a meal?"

"Restaurants are expensive," said Anna. "Come on, I'll show you where the kitchen is. You'll see I'm right."

She led us to some trench tables and benches set up outside near the doorway to a large stone building.

"This must be where the nuns live," I said. "They probably do have a big kitchen here, but I didn't know they catered to the public."

We sat down and waited. One other older-looking woman sat at the next table eating soup and bread. Shortly, a young nun came out with a platter of bread and set it down in front of us.

"Doris, this isn't a restaurant. There's no menu, and no waiters. It's a soup kitchen to feed poor people. This is kind of embarrassing."

"Maybe they'll pass a collection plate after you eat." she said. "Then maybe you won't feel embarrassed."

"You mean you're okay eating here?" I asked, with a frown.

"Well, no, but Donna and Anna are happy here."

We waited in silence, and nobody reached for the chunks of bread piled in front of us. I fidgeted and looked around to see if anyone was watching us. The old woman at the next table slurping her soup and munching her bread paid us no attention.

"This is a soup kitchen, for God's sake." And I smiled to myself at my choice of words.

"Anna," I said, "we can afford to eat at a restaurant. This is okay, but we don't want to take free food away from people who really need it."

"Many people with money eat at these places," said Anna. "But it's okay. We can leave if you want."

Just then the nun returned with a large tureen of steaming soup, and Anna told her we would not be eating there after all. The nun never said a word, just looked a little surprised, and returned to the kitchen with the soup. We got up and left.

Back on the main road we didn't see any restaurants in sight, but I remembered seeing one from the bus just before we got off. I guessed it was about a half mile beyond our rooms which were about one mile from where we stood. As we started walking down the road a horse-drawn wooden wagon with rubber tires passed us. We had seen many of these wagons in Romania, hauling everything from poles to people.

"Wouldn't it be nice if we could get a ride on one of those?" Doris asked.

Immediately, Anna ran after the wagon and stopped it. She talked to the driver a minute and waved us forward.

We all hopped into the back and enjoyed a wagon ride to the restaurant. Donna and Anna were ecstatic consulting the menu, making choices, and changing their minds. They enjoyed the experience immensely, but I thought the food was substandard and the restaurant a pretty poor place to eat. It was the only restaurant in the neighborhood but, even so, we were the only diners that evening.

The next day our grim-faced hostess fed us a breakfast of bread, butter, jam, and tea. Afterwards, the girls washed the dishes in the front yard at the hand pump, and then, cleaned up both rooms and made the beds. When we left to hike back up the road toward the monastery, our hostess waved and her grim face gave us a hint of a smile. I think she liked having young Romanian tourists.

We spent the morning hiking up a hill opposite the monastery. On the way up the girls found some mushrooms and immediately stopped to pick some to bring home to their mother.

"I hope they know which ones are safe to eat," I said.

"They probably do," said Doris, "but if they don't, their mom or Grandma Marie will."

At the top of the hill we came to a cross. Almost all the hills in Romania had some sort of object on top, such as monuments, spires, markers, or crosses. In front of this cross both girls knelt for a short prayer.

We had a good view of the monastery down below. Just before noon a cavalcade of limousines and motorcycle police arrived at the entrance to the monastery.

"That's King Carol, our king," said Donna with

excitement in her voice. "He lives in Greece, but he's come to Romania for the first time since his exile."

I looked over at Doris and shook my head slightly. I knew that King Carol had died long before these girls were born. This was probably King Michael, the son, who was exiled at the end of World War Two when the communists took over Romania. He'd be an old man by now.

"Wouldn't it be wonderful to have our King live in Romania again?" asked Donna.

"Oh yes," said Anna. "Let's go down to see if we can get close to him. Maybe he'll wave to us."

By the time we hiked down from the hill, King Carol, King Michael, or whoever he was, was gone. In his place was a portrait artist, and neither young woman spoke of King Carol again, apparently relegating him back to obscurity in favor of a good-looking man who happened to draw. They happily spent their few lei to have him draw their portraits in charcoal to give to their mother. Doris and I waited a little way from them, sitting in the shade on a stone wall.

"I'm surprised they're spending their money on portraits," I said to Doris. "We can give them lots of pictures, in color."

"It's not the same, and I'm sure their mom will like them."

"I'll tell you what," I said. "I think they're enjoying the artist's personal concentrated attention on them more than getting a drawing."

"You're probably right," said Doris. "It's not the first

time a handsome man has made women reckless with their money."

"We've got to catch our buses after these drawings are made," I called out to the young women, hoping to hurry along the picture making process. "Your mother won't like it if we don't get you back home tonight."

"And I don't want to spend another night here," I said in a low voice to Doris.

Finally, they were done and the girls proudly showed us the results.

"Very nice," said Doris, "Your mom is going to love them."

I made some appropriate comment, although I don't much care for charcoal portraits. When finished they all seemed to look alike to me. We walked back down the road, past the house we had stayed the night before, and waited at a bus stop for the bus that would take Donna and Anna home. Waiting seemed an eternity. We had already said goodbye and yet had to stand there awkwardly at the side of the road, waiting, trying to make light pleasant conversation. Each of us knew we had to part soon. *Forever.* When the bus finally came I made sure their fares were paid back to Radouti. We hugged them goodbye, again. They pleaded for us to come to their house for Christmas, and all the women cried a little. The last we saw of them were their little white hands waving to us from the window as the bus disappeared around a bend in the road.

Silently we stared a few seconds where the bus had disappeared. Then still in dead silence, Doris and I shouldered our packs, walked slowly across the road, and down to our bus stop thinking our own thoughts. There we waited patiently, still without words, for a bus to come and pick us up. Finally, Doris broke the silence.

"When will it come?"

"I don't know, but the bus dropped us off here yesterday at about this time."

"Wanna try hitchhiking?" she asked.

"Sure, but I don't think we'll get a ride. There's so little traffic on this road, and what cars do come by always seem to be packed with people."

I was wrong, again. After we stuck our thumbs in the air, the first car that came by stopped, picked us up, and delivered us over into the next valley to start another adventure.

Anna and Donna wash breakfast dishes in the front yard.

Anna and Donna picked mushrooms for their mom.)

Epilogue:
Travel Plans to Angkor Wat, Cambodia

Back in the summer of 2006, well over a year before I wanted to go, I mentioned to Doris about traveling to see Angkor Wat. I've learned you can't start too soon to promote a big trip. Once on the way, Doris loved to travel, but she would never think of initiating such a trip herself, and needed a little time to get used to the idea.

"Where's that?" she asked.

"It's in Cambodia, near Thailand. You remember how neat Thailand was?" I asked, hoping to persuade by association. It didn't work.

"Isn't that where all those people were killed? In Cambodia?"

"That was several years ago, but now it's all peaceful," I replied. "We wouldn't go if I thought it was dangerous."

That was always a major consideration for Doris

before she ever agreed to go anywhere. Me too, actually. A couple months later I mentioned Angkor Wat again.

"What is that?" she asked, showing a little more interest than before.

"It's a huge area of ancient temples and shrines, a beautiful place that rivals the Taj Mahal," I said, invoking a place she knew well, hoping again to persuade by association.

"When would you want to go?"

"I was thinking in the winter of 2007–08."

"For how long?"

Now I had to be careful. I had her interest, but she usually objects to a trip when she thinks it's too long.

"I'm not sure. I'll have to figure it out," I said, giving myself more time.

A few weeks later, I brought the subject up again.

"You know I've been looking into going to Angkor Wat, but that area has so many other wonderful places to see, like Laos and Vietnam. If we go to see Angkor Wat, we might just as well see them, too," I mentioned casually.

"If we did all that, how long would we be gone?" *Doris, sure loves her home.*

"To see all three countries might take a couple weeks or more," I said.

Doris likes to talk to friends and strangers and soon she received glowing accounts from other people who had been to Indochina. In the meantime, I just happened to receive a tour company brochure in the mail featuring trips to Indochina from ten days up to twenty days. I inquired about the twenty-day trip, of course. Its cost was $3,800, including airfare, and would start the sixth of January and end the twenty-fifth of January, 2008. Not counting the days of travel getting there and back gave us an actual tour of seventeen days. I thought that was pretty expensive until I asked around and found that the cost was competitive.

When I told Doris about the tour, she didn't even mention cost.

"You know I hate guided tours," she said. "Couldn't we do it on our own?"

"I thought about it, but I think it would be difficult for us to do on our own in those countries. Especially, since I'm so darn weak anymore."

Doris grudgingly agreed to a tour. *Hot dogs, we were going.* About April, 2007, I called the tour company and nailed down a spot for us on their tour starting from Seattle on the sixth of January, and agreed to send them a seven hundred dollar deposit for two. A few weeks later I pushed the envelope with Doris again.

"You know, we'll be very close to India when we go on this tour. I would like to see that country again, and I know you like that place a lot, too. It's so expensive getting over to that area, we might as well stay a little longer to see India, and mitigate the cost of the airfare."

"I would love to go to India," she said. "Would we go before or after Angkor Wat?"

"Well, I was thinking that the Indochina tour lasts most of January, so it might be best to go to India in

December, starting maybe on the fifteenth. I think it might get too hot if we went to India in February."

"So, how long would we be away?" she asked. *A one-track mind.*

"We'd be in India on our own for a good three weeks before our tour starts, and then on the guided tour for three weeks. That's six weeks."

"Oh, we've been away longer than that on trips," said Doris with disdain in her voice, while waving a hand back over her shoulder. "That's no problem."

It's full steam ahead, I thought. *Yea, hooray!*

Since the Indochina tour included round-trip airfare to Bangkok, not India, I asked the tour people for a quote of land price, only. That's when I found out what I had missed in their fine print. Airfare included in their price was from LA back to LA. I had to find and pay my own way from Seattle to LA and back. But now, it didn't matter since we were going to India directly from Seattle, and would join up with our tour in Bangkok on the eighth of January instead of the sixth.

Also in the fine print was a blurb about a minimum. The tour wouldn't go unless ten people signed up for the trip. That was kind of worrisome, but hey, the trip didn't start until 6 January, seven months ahead. Surely other people would sign up for such a neat trip.

The next step was getting plane tickets from Seattle to India and back. I browsed the Internet and found an outfit called "JustFares." They soon set me straight on the difficulty of traveling at Christmas time.

"Haven't you ever heard of Christmas?" asked Abraham, the agent in charge of getting me plane tickets.

"Sure," I said, "but Christmas isn't until the twenty-fifth, and we're leaving the fifteenth. Besides, those people over there don't celebrate our holidays."

"I don't know about that," he said, "but the airlines are sold out of cheap seats; every one of them gone for the month of December."

"But this is only June, for God's sake."

"I know," he said. "I can probably find you something if you're prepared to pay an arm and a leg."

"I don't have any extra arms or legs," I responded. "What can we do?"

"Change your schedule a little, and leave earlier," said Abraham. "Let me check around, and see what I can do."

The best that Abraham could do was to reserve seats to leave Seattle, November 29. Fly to Bangalore, India; then from Mumbai to Bangkok on the first of January in plenty of time to meet our tour to Indochina; and then home from there on the twenty-fifth. *Change my schedule a little? Good grief, leaving Seattle before December was a lot, not a little.*

"Do it," I said, and paid the price of $1,450 for each ticket.

I felt very discouraged, like I had screwed up in some way. I had saved the cost of airfare to Bangkok, $642—by paying only the cost of the land portion of the guided tour, yet I had just paid out an awful lot more than that to get to Southeast Asia. I sat down and doodled with a few figures as follows:

Airfare, Seattle-India-Bangkok-Seattle by JustFares_$1450
Airfare saved from guided tour package cost_____$642
Airfare round trip, Seattle-LA-Seattle_____$250
Airfare round trip, Bangkok - India–Bangkok_____$400
Taxes and surcharge_____$120
*Total*_____$1412

Although I had guessed at the cost of the second set of figures, I thought they wouldn't be too far off from the actual cost. In any event, I felt better about the price I had paid to JustFares for airplane tickets.

    I spent many days reading the Lonely Planet guidebook to India to gain enough knowledge to make a suitable itinerary. We were flying into Southern India to Bangalore, and out of India at Mumbai. So, I made a tentative list of places I wanted to see stretching from Bangalore to Mumbai and an additional loop from Mumbai to Agra and back. I had to go to Agra, the site of the most beautiful structure I've ever seen, the Taj Mahal. Then I assigned consecutive days to each place I wanted to see, and ended up with a trip of at least sixty days. Darn airline reservation dates. They constrained me to a trip of about thirty days. It took me hours to figure out which places to leave in the itinerary and which to leave out.

    Doris wasn't too much help either. She doesn't think about the places we go until we get there, and then thoroughly enjoys the moment. I, on the other hand, ponder and deliberate on all the possibilities even after we start the trip. So, the itinerary is meant to be somewhat flexible. I just never want to be in a strange place and wonder why we're there, and then scramble to figure out what to see and do after we arrive.

I found that traveling back to a place I've seen before can be disappointing. Places change and memories of those places may not be realistic. I'd been to India three times, and the temptation to see again some of those wonderful places in my memory was tempting. My solution was to mix new places evenly with those I'd seen before.

Doris and I seldom traveled by plane once we got to the area we planned to visit. We went by public ground transport. It was buses in South America, trains in Europe, and a combination of trucks, buses, and a rented car in Africa. Our choice in India was trains. Specifically, the second-class trains. They went to every nook and cranny of the county, day and night, and were dirt cheap for us to use. In that way we also got to interact with the people we came so far to see.

In August, I contacted the tour company that was providing us the Indochina trip. They had four people signed up for the tour, including Doris and me. I was fretting about the ten people rule; I didn't want to chance the tour not happening. That meant we'd be stuck in Thailand with time on our hands and nowhere to go. Of course, I assumed we could change our tickets to come home sooner without visiting Indochina, but I didn't like that idea. Besides, it was bound to be costly. In addition, we had some free time from the first of January when we arrived in Bangkok, until the eighth of January when we joined our tour to see Angkor Wat.

That's when I went browsing on the Internet. I wanted to see if other tours were available if ours didn't go. I found lots of tours, but none quite as good as the one we had. Then I stumbled onto a tour company in Vietnam called Threeland Tours. They had tours that went from Bangkok-Laos-Vietnam-Cambodia-Bangkok for one to twenty people, leaving Bangkok anytime we wished.

"They have a tour going to the countries I want to see," I said to Doris, "and I think they'll take just the two of us. Amazing."

"I would like that better than going with a group of strangers," she said with some excitement showing in her voice. "Cancel the other tour."

Doris always liked to get things done right now, but instead, I contacted Threeland by email. I asked them for an itinerary and a quote for a three country tour to start in Bangkok on 1 January and end there on 25 January for two persons. Back came the reply the next day. *Quick, on the ball. Good.* They sent me a complete five-page detailed itinerary, and invited me to make changes if I desired. The cost was just under three thousand dollars each, which was considerably less cost per day than the tour I had signed up with.

"Cancel that other tour," said Doris.

Their price included all flights in and among the three countries, a car and driver, a guide, and all hotel costs, all meals, all entry fees at various sights, and at least five boat excursions. Drinks, visa costs, and tips were at our expense.

"You've got to cancel that other tour," said Doris again.

She and I had different time schedules for getting things done, which drove her crazy sometimes. My theory involved waiting until the last moment, because many times problems fixed themselves without me ever lifting a finger. Besides, I still had to finalize the itinerary and agree to their proposed costs.

I wrote back to Threeland that I wanted to eliminate from their itinerary; visits to killing fields, war monuments, military tunnels, torture chambers, and anything having to do with the Vietnam War. I think I let my prejudice show a little, but I figured the trip was our vacation, not a trip to remind us of war. We didn't visit Auschwitz, either, when in Poland, opting to see the salt mines instead.

"We want to interact with the people, and see how they live and work," I wrote. "To see more countryside and people, please substitute overland trips for two of the scheduled airplane flights. Also, we wish to find our own restaurants and pay for them separately."

Back came the reply: "Okay, okay, no problem. We suggest an allowance of fifteen dollars per person per day for meals. Attached is your final itinerary, and the cost remains the same."

I didn't wait for Doris to remind me again. I called and cancelled the tour we had signed up for, and received a total refund of our deposit. I don't think that trip was going to happen anyway. I knew that going to India and Indochina was going to cost a bunch, but I didn't know how much. Some of the costs were pre-paid before we left home, but we needed to know how many dollars to take with us. So, I made some estimates of cost to determine how much cash each of us should bring along.

India Trip: Cash on Hand Required Per Person

Lodging; not counting overnight trains, 26 nights @ $20 each night	$520
Meals; 30 days @ $20 each day	$600
Drinks; (water, beer, soda) 30 days @ $10 each day	$300
Trains and buses; 18 trips @ $5 each trip	$90
Overnight trains; 4 trips @ $10 each trip	$40
Taxi; 40 trips @ $1.50 each trip	$60
Entry fees and gratuities	$120
Visa	$60
Misc. and extra	$173
Total for India	$2000

Indochina Trip: Cash on Hand Required Per Person

Visa	$107
Meals; 24 days @ $15 each day	$360
Drinks; 24 days @ $10 each day	$240
Airport Taxes	$70
Taxi; 10 trips @ $5 each trip	$50
Misc. and Extras	$173
Total for Indochina	$1000

Doris and I had learned by experience that traveling with light backpacks was much more fun than horsing around with heavy, bulky suitcases, even those with the little wheels and collapsible dragging handles. Besides, when we got older we couldn't carry a bunch of weight around anyway. We tried to keep our packs weighing in at about twenty pounds. That was a fairly easy amount to carry, and hoist up onto overhead racks on trains and buses.

Once I asked Doris, "How come your pack always looks so overstuffed? Are you gaining weight?"

"I'm not gaining weight and neither is my pack," she said glaring over at me. "Here, lift it and see for yourself."

Of course, I couldn't judge the weight of her pack.

"I'll take it and put it on the scale," I said.

"No you won't," she said grabbing the pack out of my hand. "I'll never ask you to carry any of my stuff, so forget it." *Maybe she's an untidy packer, and leaves lots of spaces around her clothes.*

For this trip, aside from what we wear on the plane, we will each carry the following: three shirts, one pair of pants, three changes of underwear and socks, one light wool sweater and sun hat, one very light windbreaker with hood, pills and medicines (these get heavier as the years go by), first-aid stuff, minimum toiletries, including a roll of toilet paper, which Doris uses at a prolific rate and then starts borrowing mine when hers is gone (*How can a person borrow toilet paper?*), shaving gear for me, a light full-length wraparound skirt for Doris, a silk underwear top that Doris never leaves home without, a half-dozen small nylon or silk scarves for Doris which she uses to vary her outfit, masking the fact that she's worn the same shirt for days, and extra stuff that Doris sneaks into her pack thinking I won't notice.

Occasionally we'll wash underwear and socks in our hotel room along the way. But almost all hotels have someone willing to do laundry at a reasonable price. When our shirts and pants finally get dirty enough, we send everything out to be washed, and start off again with all our clothes squeaky clean. We didn't expect to find laundromats on this trip.

Doris always carts a little daypack around with her on these trips. I've tried several times to convince her not to encumber herself with that extra pack, but now I think it's psychological. She's so used to dragging a purse around with her at home that she feels uncomfortable with nothing in her hand. I can't complain too much, for out of that little pack comes snacks, bottled water, toilet paper, sun hats, crossword-puzzle books, paper and pen; and my insulin stuffed in a chemical pack that keeps it cool enough so it won't go bad on hot days.

Now, the major work of planning the trip was done. A few things remained to do such as:

1) Send away for India visas.

2) Reserve a hotel room in Bangalore, since we arrived there about midnight

3) Reserve sleeper space on the overnight train out of Bangalore. We wanted to leave the next night and the seats had to be reserved several days in advance.

Doris and I at home between trips.

4) Visit the travel doctor and get shot-up.

5) Buy one hundred dollars worth of Indian rupees to have on hand when we arrived.

6) Save up some money and go.

A rhyme came to mind from my childhood days long, long ago.

> One for the money,
> Two for the show,
> Three to get ready,
> And four to *Go*.

And go we did. I in my seventy-eighth year, and Doris in her seventy-ninth year.

listen|imagine|view|experience

AUDIO BOOK DOWNLOAD INCLUDED WITH THIS BOOK!

In your hands you hold a complete digital entertainment package. Besides purchasing the paper version of this book, this book includes a free download of the audio version of this book. Simply use the code listed below when visiting our website. Once downloaded to your computer, you can listen to the book through your computer's speakers, burn it to an audio CD or save the file to your portable music device (such as Apple's popular iPod) and listen on the go!

How to get your free audio book digital download:

1. Visit www.tatepublishing.com and click on the e|LIVE logo on the home page.
2. Enter the following coupon code:
   b011-71d4-6ceb-f5b7-4b07-467a-b2a8-fea7
3. Download the audio book from your e|LIVE digital locker and begin enjoying your new digital entertainment package today!

listen|imagine|view|experience

AUDIO BOOK DOWNLOAD INCLUDED WITH THIS BOOK!

In your hands you hold a complete digital entertainment package. Besides purchasing the paper version of this book, this book includes a free download of the audio version of this book. Simply use the code listed below when visiting our website. Once downloaded to your computer, you can listen to the book through your computer's speakers, burn it to an audio CD or save the file to your portable music device (such as Apple's popular iPod) and listen on the go!

How to get your free audio book digital download:

1. Visit www.tatepublishing.com and click on the e|LIVE logo on the home page.
2. Enter the following coupon code:
   b011-71d4-6ceb-f5b7-4b07-467a-b2a8-fea7
3. Download the audio book from your e|LIVE digital locker and begin enjoying your new digital entertainment package today!